**Strange people in the
worlds of Theodore Sturgeon . . .**

The woman who kept mad, blind faith in the
goodness of her lover—a man who was betray-
ing the whole world to the forces of ultimate
destruction.

The biochemist who desperately tried to control
the drug he had invented—a chemical that
turned love into a killer disease that would
ravage the planet.

The creature from space that committed suicide
out of affection for the human being whose mind
he had invaded.

And others, uniquely memorable, fascinatingly
unexpected.

STURGEON IN ORBIT

Theodore Sturgeon

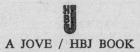

A JOVE / HBJ BOOK

TO THE MOST PATIENT OF ALL EDITORS, WHO IS OUTSHOWN
BY PERKINS ONLY FOR HIS LACK OF A WOLF
DON BENSEN
AND HIS LOVELY ANNE.

First Jove/HBJ edition published January 1978

Printed in the United States of America

ACKNOWLEDGMENTS

EXTRAPOLATION, originally published in Fantastic as BE-
   WARE THE FURY. Copyright 1953 by Ziff-Davis Publish-
   ing Company.
MAKE ROOM FOR ME, originally published in Fantastic Ad-
   ventures. Copyright 1951 by Ziff-Davis Publishing Company.
THE INCUBI OF PARALLEL X, originally published in
   Planet Stories. Copyright 1951 by Fiction House, Inc.
THE WAGES OF SYNERGY, originally published in Startling
   Stories, August, 1953. Copyright 1953 by Better Publications,
   Inc.
THE HEART, originally published in Other Worlds, May 1955.
   Copyright 1955 Greenleaf Publishing Co.

Jove/HBJ books are published by Jove Publications, Inc. (Harcourt Brace Jovanovich), 757 Third Avenue, New York, N.Y.
10017

CONTENTS

5

Introduction

As the observant reader will already have discovered, this book is dedicated to, and in a way is about, editors.

Editors are a strange breed, and anyone who makes a sweeping statement, expecting it to include them all, is bound to be wrong. Editors are also at the blade end of many a slashing wisecrack, like the one which says an editor is a writer who couldn't make it (and an agent is a writer who couldn't make it as an editor). "An editor," one writer told me years ago when I had bloom on my down, "is just something which rhymes with creditor. They're both out to get you."

I have had editors who have been simultaneously my best friends and my worst enemies. One editor once complained about the return postage I attached to my manuscripts: "Who can find any use for a 20¢ stamp? Make it up in twos and threes—" (this was some time ago) "—so I can get some use out of them." This was when I first realized that when an editor buys a story, he expects you to be so thrilled with the check you'll overlook the fact that you didn't get your postage back. Fabulous exception: Don Ward, who always clipped the stamps to the check, and then sent same airmail.

I've had an editor monstrously fond of changing my stories—not in the ordinary run of editorial nuts-and-bolts, for all stories which sell to periodicals must be made to fit available space, but just because he could not bear to leave one alone. I never realized how desperate a need this was in him until one day he begged me not to get an electric typewriter: "The damn things make such a beautiful page I can't bring myself to touch them with a blue pencil." For all that, once I'd had it out with him, I began the practice of writing 'stet' (a printer's term meaning 'run as is') in the margins beside whatever phrasing I thought he might like to change; and I will say he never violated that. And once I had an editor push a whole pile of manuscripts back at me:

7

his lips were rage-white and he was trembling, and he said he would never buy a story from a man who wrote the likes of *Bianca's Hands* (which is not in this book, by the way).

Yet there are editors who try their sizable utmost to discover what a writer is *for*—why he is what he is, and what he can do to make that unique something (we are all unique, you know) important. I've had an editor who had every reason to stomp me dead and sue me besides for being late with a story, write me and say, "I ought to have my head examined for telling you this, but it matters more that you write the way you want to than that I meet my deadlines. You take your time." I've had editors send me their personal checks to help me through a tight squeeze when their offices couldn't be persuaded to make an advance. I've had letters of comment on a short-story which ran up to twelve single-spaced pages—actually more words than the story itself—because some editor was excited about a possibility raised by the manuscript. I've had one editor pass a story of mine on to another, when the first couldn't buy it and the second could. And by and large editors are an uncomplaining lot. You know, the most I have ever been able to spend for a typewriter ribbon was $2.79—you can find them for as little as half a dollar. Yet writers perpetually write their ribbons to the palest grey, and editors, who depend on their eyesight for a livelihood, perpetually accept and read copy that a grocery clerk would refuse to read off a shopping list. In all the years I've been writing, I've heard of only one editor who returned a manuscript (not mine!) unread for this reason—and more power to him, say I.

As a writer who has been involved in films, TV, radio, books and magazines, and who has therefore encountered many different kinds of editors, I depose and say that the most important communion a writer can have is between himself and his words. The man who intervenes least in this rather sacred process is the magazine editor, especially the small magazine editor who is his own staff. When he really does know what a writer is *for*, when he counsels wisely and and mends invisibly, he is a pearl of great price. If you find one, stick with him, even at a penny a word, even if you're selling elsewhere for thousands. He is worth your loyalty.

This might be called a "forgotten" story in the sense that it has, through the years, been overlooked by anthologists and yet (I have it on good authority) is one of my major works. I know that when I unearthed it for this volume and read it, I put it down with (incredibly) real tears in my eyes. I let Groff Conklin (now there's a good editor) see it, and he confessed it had him weeping aloud. It was Howard Browne who bought this story, and I suddenly recall the circumstances, because it was the only time such a thing ever happened to me. I came in with it and said, "Look, Howard, I'd appreciate it if you could let me know on this sort of soon because—" He interrupted me: "You in a bind? Wait a minute." He reached for the phone and said "Accounting Department?" Then to me, "How long is it?" I told him. Howard looked up at the ceiling for a moment, calculating, and then said into the phone, "Send up a check for Theodore Sturgeon for a story called Extrapolation *for (he named a figure)." "But Howard!" I cried, "you haven't read it yet!" He shrugged his Kodiak-bear shoulders. "I don't need to and you know it."*

They don't hardly make 'em like that no more.

Extrapolation

"READ IT FOR yourself," said the Major.

She took the sheaf of flimsies from him and for a moment gave him that strange dry gaze. *The woman's in shock,* he thought, and did what he could to put down the other two memories he had of eyes like that: an injured starling which had died in his hand; his four-year-old niece, the time he struck her, and the long unbearable moment between the impact and her tears.

Mrs. Reger read carefully and slowly. Her face slept. Her eyes reflected and would not transmit. Her long hands were more vulnerable. The Major heard the whisper of the thin paper; then she turned far enough away from him to steady the backs of her fingers against the mantel. When at last she was finished she put the report down on the black coffee table gently, gently, as if it might shatter. They stood together looking down on it and its blue blare of stamp-pad ink: TOP SECRET.

She said, at last, "That is the foulest thing a human being has ever done." Then her mouth slept again.

"I'm glad you agree," he said. "I was afraid that—" and then she was looking at him again and he could not go on.

"I don't think I understand you," she said tonelessly. "You meant the report. I thought you meant Wolf Reger."

"That's what I was afraid of," he said.

She glanced down at the report. "That isn't Wolf. Wolf might be a lot of things . . . things that are . . . hard to understand. But he isn't a traitor." The Major saw her face lifting and turned his head to avoid those hurt eyes. "I think," she said quietly, "that you'd better go, Major, and take those lies with you."

He made no move toward the report. "Mrs. Reger," he suddenly shouted, "do you think I'm enjoying this? Do you think I volunteered for this job?"

"I hadn't thought about you at all."

"Try it," he said bitterly. Then, "Sorry. I'm sorry. This whole thing . . ." He pulled himself together. "I wish I could believe you. But you've got to realize that a man died to make that report and get it back to us. We have no choice but to take it for the truth and act accordingly. What else can we do?"

"Do what you like. But don't ask me to believe things about my husband that just aren't so."

Watching her, he felt that if she lost that magnificent control it would be more than he could bear. *God*, he thought, *where did a rat like Reger ever find such a woman?* As gently as he could, he said, "Very well, Mrs. Reger. You needn't believe it. . . . May I tell you exactly what my assignment is?"

She did not answer.

He said, "I was detailed to get from you everything which might have any bearing on—on this report." He pointed. "Whether I believe it or not is immaterial. Perhaps if you can tell me enough about the man, I won't believe it. Perhaps," he said, knowing his voice lacked conviction, "we can clear him. Wouldn't you help clear him?"

"He doesn't need clearing," she said impatiently. Then, when he made a tiny, exasperated sound, she said, "I'll help you. What do you want to know?"

All the relief, all the gratitude, and all the continuing distaste for this kind of work were in his voice. "Everything.

Why he might do a thing like that." And, quickly, "Or why he wouldn't."

She told him about Wolf Reger, the most hated man on earth.

*

Beware the fury of a patient man.

Wolf Reger had so many talents that they were past enumerating. With them he had two characteristics which were extreme. One was defenselessness. The other was an explosive anger which struck without warning, even to Reger himself.

His defenselessness sprang from his excess of ability. When blocked, it was all too easy for him to excel in some other field. It was hard to make him care much for anything. Rob him, turn him, use him—it didn't matter. In a day, a week, he could find something better. For this he was robbed, and turned, and used.

His anger was his only terror. When he was eight he was chasing another boy—it was fun; they ran and laughed and dodged through the boy's large old house. And at the very peak of hilarity, the other boy ran outside and slammed the french doors in Wolf's face and stood grinning through the glass. Wolf instantly hit the face with his fist. The double-thick glass shattered. Wolf severed two tendons and an artery in his wrist, and the other boy fell gasping, blood from his carotid spurting between his futile fingers. The boy was saved, but the effect on Wolf was worse than if he had died. His anger had lasted perhaps three microseconds, and when it was gone, it was gone completely. So brief a thing could hardly be termed a madness—not even a blindness. But it left the boy with the deep conviction that one day this lightning would strike and be gone, and he would find himself looking at a corpse.

He never ran and shouted again. He lived every moment of the next four years under the pressure of his own will, holding down what he felt was an internal devil, analyzing every situation he met for the most remote possibility of its coming to life again. With that possibility visualized, he would avoid the situation. He therefore avoided sandlot baseball and school dances; competitions and group activities; friendship. He did very well with his school work. He did very badly with his fellows.

When he was twelve he met a situation he could not avoid. He was in his second year of high-school then, and every day for three weeks a bulky sophomore twice his size would catch him on his way from English to Geometry II, wrap a thick arm around his neck, and grind a set of knuckles into his scalp. Wolf took it and took it, and one day he tore himself free and struck. He was small and thin, and the chances are that the surprise of the attack was more effective than its power. Their legs were entangled and the bigger boy was off balance. He hit the tile floor with his head and lay quite still with his lips white and blood trickling from his ear. For six weeks they did not know if he would live or not. Wolf was expelled from school the day it happened, and never went to another. From that point on he never dared be angry.

It was easy to hate Wolf Reger. He surpassed anyone he worked with and was disliked for it. He retreated from anyone who wanted what he had, and was despised for it. He communicated but would not converse. He immediately and forcefully rejected any kind of companionship, apparently because he did not need it, but actually because he did not dare let anyone come close to him. And his basic expertness was extrapolation—the ability to project every conceivable factor in a situation to every possible conclusion. He chose his work this way. He chose his restaurants this way, his clothes—everything he did and was. He lived to avoid others for their own protection.

He had two great successes—one a chemical process and one an electronic device. They taught him enough about fame to frighten him away from it. Fame meant people, meetings, associates. After that he let others take the credit for the work he did.

At thirty he was married.

*

"Why?"

The question hung offensively in the air between them for an appreciable time before the Major realized that he had spoken it aloud and incredulously.

She said, carefully, "Major, what have you in your notebook so far?"

He looked down at the neat rows of symbols. "A few facts. A few conjectures."

With an accuracy that shook him in his chair, she said coldly, "You have him down as a warped little genius with every reason to hate humanity. If I weren't sure of that, I wouldn't go on with this. Major," she said suddenly in a different voice, "suppose I told you that I was walking down the street and a man I had never seen before suddenly roared at me, leapt on my back, knocked me down, beat me and rolled me in the gutter. Suppose you had fifty eyewitnesses who would swear it happened. What would you think of the man?"

He looked at her sleek hair, her strong, obedient features. Despite himself he felt a quixotic anger toward her attacker, even in hypothesis. "Isn't it obvious? The man would have to be a drunk, a psychopath. At the very least he would have to be deluded, think you were someone else. Even if he did, only a real skunk would do a thing like that to a woman." He suddenly realized how easily she had pulled him away from his subject, and was annoyed. "What has this to do—"

"You'll see." She captured his gaze, and he had the sensation that for the very first time she was examining him, looking at his eyes, his mouth; looking at him as a man instead of an unavoidable talking-machine in uniform. "I hope you'll see," she said thoughtfully. Then, "You wanted to know why he married me."

The Army wants to know that, he corrected silently. *I'd like to know why you married him.*

*

She committed suicide.

Relentlessly she told the Major why, and he put his pencil down until she had finished with that part of the story. This was a report on Reger, not on his wife. Her reasons were good, at the time, and they constituted a tale of disillusion and defeat which has been, and will be, told again and again.

She stumbled out into the desert and walked until she dropped; until she was sure there could be no rescue; until she had barely strength to lift the phial and drink. She regained consciousness eight months later, in civilian married quarters at Space Base Two. She had been dead twice.

It was a long time before she found out what had happened. Reger, who would not permit himself to move about among people, took his exercise at night, and found her; she had walked almost to the Base without knowing it, and Reger all but tripped over her body. It was not a small body, and he was not a large man, but somehow he got her back to his quarters, a one-room and bath affair as near to the edge of the housing area as it could be and still be in the Base. She was still alive—barely.

How he saved her, no one but Reger could know. He knew she was drugged or poisoned, and exhausted. He found the right medication to keep her from slipping further away, but for weeks he could not bring her back. He did the job for which he was hired, and he worked over her as well, and no one knew she was there. Twice her heart stopped and he started it again, once with adrenalin and once with electric shock.

Her autonomic nervous system was damaged. When she began to convalesce, he started drug therapy. He kept her paralyzed and at the edge of unconsciousness, so that the slow business of repair could proceed without hindrance. He fed her intravenously.

And still he kept his job, and no one knew.

And then one day there was a knock on his door. One room and bath; to open the door was to open the whole room to an outsider. He ignored the knock and it came again, and then again, timidly but insistently. He extrapolated, as always, and disliked his conclusion. A woman in his bachelor quarters created a situation which could only mean people and people, talk and talk—and the repeated, attenuated annoyance which, of all things, he feared most.

He picked her up and carried her into the bathroom and shut the door. Then he answered the knock. It was nothing important—a chirping little bird of a woman who was taking up a collection for a Thanksgiving party for the orphans in town. He wrote her a check and got rid of her, snarling suddenly that she must never bother him again—and pass the word. That, and the size of the check, took care of her and anyone like her.

He nearly collapsed from reaction after she had gone. He knew he could not possibly outguess the exigencies which might arise to bring other people on other errands. A power failure, a fire, even curious boys or a peeping Tom; the law of averages dictated that in spite of his reputation for being a recluse, in spite of the isolation of his quarters, somebody had to discover his secret. She had been with him for four months now. How could he explain her? Doctors would know she had been under treatment for some time; the Air Force people at the Base, and their cackling wives, would make God only knew what sort of racket about it.

So he married her.

It took another six weeks to build her up sufficiently to be moved. He drove her to a town a hundred and fifty miles away and married her in a hotel room. She was under a skilfully applied hypnotic, and carefully instructed. She knew nothing about it at the time and remembered nothing afterward. Reger then applied for married quarters, moved her back to the Base and continued her therapy. Let them pry. He had married and his bride was not only ill, but as anti-social as he.

*

"There's your androphobe," said Mrs. Reger. "He could have let me die. He could have turned me over to the doctors."

"You're a very attractive woman," he pointed out. "You were that, plus a challenge . . . two kinds of challenge. Could he keep you alive? Could he do it while doing his job? A man who won't compete with people generally finds something else to pit himself against."

"You're quite impartial while you wait for all the facts," she said bitterly.

"No I'm not," he said, and quite astonished himself by adding, "It's just that I can't lie to you." There was a slight emphasis on the last word which he wished he could go back and erase.

She let it pass and went on with her story.

*

She must have had consciousness of a sort long before he was aware of it. She was born again, slowly, aware of comfort and safety, an alternation of light and dark, a dim appreciation of the way in which her needs were met, a half-conscious anticipation of his return when she found herself alone.

He surrounded her with music—the automatic phonograph when he was away, the piano when he was home and not busy. Music was his greatest escape, and he escaped deeply into it. She had been musical all her life, and recognized an astonishing sensitivity in the silent man. Security and the wordless reaches of music broadened her consciousness from a thin line to a wide swath, forward and back, past and future. The more she fumbled her way back, the more she appreciated her present, and the more it mystified her. Because of this she lay quiet for many days when she could have spoken to him, trying to understand. When at last she was ready, she frightened him badly. She had never dreamed that anyone could be quite so shy, so self-abasing. She had not known that a human being could dislike himself so much. Yet he had an inner strength and unlimited resourcefulness. He was completely efficient in everything he did except in his effort to talk with her.

He told her, with terror in his eyes, of their marriage, and he begged her pardon for it. It was as if a harsh word from her would destroy him. And she smiled and thanked him. He went silently away and sat down at the piano, though he did not play it again while she was there.

She convalesced very quickly after that. She tried her very best to understand him. She succeeded in making him talk about himself, and was careful not to help him, ever, nor to work with him at anything. He never touched her. She divined that he never should, until he was quite ready, and so she never forced the issue. She fell completely in love with him.

At the time the *Starscout* was in the ways, and they were running final tests on it. Reger was forced to spend more and more time out at the gantry area. Sometimes he would work fifty or sixty consecutive hours, and though she hated to see him stumble home, drawn and tired, she looked forward to these times. For in his deepest sleep, she could tiptoe into his room and sit near and watch his face, study it with the stiffness of control gone, find in it the terrified eight-year-old with blood spouting from his wrist, watching a playmate with a cut throat. She could isolate the poet, the painter in him, speaking and creating and expressing only in music, for words and shapes could not be trusted. She loved him. She could wait. Those who love love, and those who love themselves, cannot wait. Those who love another can and do. So she watched him silently and tiptoed out when he stirred.

His extrapolations never ceased, and he was aware before she was that, not being a Wolf Reger, her needs were different from his. He suggested that she walk in the sun when he was away. He told her where the commissary was, and left money for shopping. She did as he expected her to do.

Then he didn't come back from the gantry area any more, and when the fifty or sixty hours got to be seventy and eighty, she made up her mind to find him. She knew quite a few people at the Base by that time. She walked in, stopping at the post office on the way. The divorce papers were waiting for her there.

*

The Major dropped his pencil.

"You didn't know about that."

"Not yet. We'd have found out anyway." He stooped, groping for the pencil, and cracked his head noisily on the coffee table. He demanded, "Why? Why did he divorce you?"

"He didn't. He filed suit. It has to be put on the court calendar and then heard, and then adjudicated, and then there's a ninety-day wait . . . you know. I went to a dance."

"A—oh." He understood that this was in answer to his question. "He divorced you because you went to a dance?"

"No! . . . well, yes." She closed her eyes. "I used to go to the Base movie once in a while when Wolf was working. I went down there and there was a dance going on instead. I sat with one of the women from the commissary and watched, and after a while her husband asked me to dance. I did. I knew Wolf would have let me if he'd been there—not that he ever would.

"And I happened to glance through the door as we danced past, and Wolf was standing just outside. His face . . ."

She rose and went to the mantel. She put out her hand very slowly, watching it move, and trailed the tips of her fingers along the polished wood. "All twisted. All . . .

"As soon as the music stopped," she whispered, "I ran out to him. He was still there."

The Major thought, *Don't break, for God's sake don't. Not while I'm here.*

"Extrapolation," she said. "Everything he saw, he computed and projected. I was dancing. I suppose I was smiling. Wolf never learned to dance, Major. Can you imagine how important that can be to a man who can do anything?

"When I got outside he was just the same as always, quiet and controlled. What he was going through inside, I hate to think. We walked home and the only thing that was said was when I told him I was sorry. He looked at me with such astonishment that I didn't dare say anything else. Two days later he left."

"On the *Starscout*. Didn't you know he was a crew-member?"

"No. I found out later. Wolf had so many skills that he

was nine-tenths of a crew all by himself. They'd wanted him for the longest time, but he'd always refused. I guess because he couldn't bear sharing space with someone."

"He did, with you."

"Did he?"

The major did not answer. She said, "That was going to end. He was sure of that. It could end any time. But space flight's something else again."

"Why did he divorce you?"

She seemed to shake herself awake. "Have I been talking out loud?" she asked.

"What? Yes!"

"Then I've told you."

"Perhaps you have," he conceded. He poised his pencil.

"What are you going to write?" When he would not answer, she said, "Not telling the truth any more, Major?"

"Not now," he said firmly.

For the second time she gave him that searching inspection, really seeing him. "I wonder what you're thinking," she murmured.

He wrote, closed the book and rose. "Thank you very much for cooperating like this," he said stiffly.

She nodded. He picked up his hat and went to the door. He opened it, hesitated, closed it again. "Mrs. Reger—"

She waited, unbelievably still—her body, her mouth.

"In your own words—why did he file suit?"

She almost smiled. "You think my words are better than what you wrote?" Then, soberly, "He saw me dancing and it hurt him. He was shocked to the core. He hadn't known it would hurt. He hadn't realized until then that he loved me. He couldn't face that—he was afraid we might be close. And one day he'd lose his temper, and I'd be dead. So he went out into space."

"Because he loved you."

"Because he loved me enough," she said quietly.

He looked away from her because he must, and saw the report still lying on the coffee table. "I'd better take this along."

"Oh yes, do." She picked it up, handed it to him. "It's the same thing as that story I told you—about the man knocking me down."

"Man—oh. Yes, that one. What was that about?"

"It really happened," she said. "He knocked me down and beat me, right in broad daylight, in front of witnesses, and everything I said about it is true."

"Bastard," growled the Major, and then blushed like a girl. "I'm sorry."

She did smile, this time. "There was a loading-dock there, in front of a warehouse. A piece of machinery in a crate got loose and slid down a chute toward the street. It hit a drum of gasoline and struck a spark. The first thing I knew, I was all over flames. That man knocked me down and beat them out with his bare hands. He saved my life."

Slowly, his jaw dropped. She said, "It makes a difference, when you know all the facts, doesn't it? Even when the first facts you got are all true?" She rapped the TOP SECRET stamp with her fingernails. "I said this was all a lie. Well, maybe it's all true. But if it is, it's like the first part of that little story. You need the rest of it. I don't. You don't know Wolf Reger. I do. Goodbye, Major."

*

He sat in his office at Headquarters and slowly pounded the fresh copy of his transcribed notes. *I have to send them the way they are,* he thought, and *but I can't. I can't.*

He swore violently and got up. He went to the watercooler, punched out a paper cup, filled it, and hurled it into the wastebasket. *All I have is facts. She has faith.*

The world was full of women, and a perfectly normal percentage of them were capable of knocking him for a loop. He wasn't immune. But surely he was old enough and wise enough by now not to let it interfere with facts. Especially in this case. If the world knew what was in that TOP SECRET report, the world would know how to feel about Wolf Reger. And then Reger's wife would be one against three and a quarter billion. How could a man in his right mind worry about a choice, with odds like that?

He cursed again and snatched up his briefcase, unlocked it, and took out the secret report. He slammed it down on top of his transcript. *One more look. One more look at the facts.*

He read:

This is the fourth time I've erased this tape and now I got no time for officialese if I'm going to get it all on here. A tape designed for hull-inspection reports in space wasn't designed for a description of a planetary invasion. But that's what it's got to be. So, for the record, this is Jerry Wain, Starscout navigator, captive on one of the cruisers that's going to invade Earth. First contact with extra-terrestrials.

Supposed to be a great moment in human history. Likely to be one of the last moments too.

The Starscout's *gone and Minelli, Joe Cook, and the Captain are dead. That leaves me and that bastard Reger. The aliens had us bracketed before we knew it, out past Jupiter. They cut up the 'scout with some sort of field or something that powdered the hull in lines as broad as your hand. No heat, no impact. Just fine powder, and she fell apart. Joe never got to a suit. The Captain went forward to stay with the ship, I guess, and couldn't have lived long after they sliced the dome off the control room. The three of us got clear and they took us in. They cut Minelli up to see what his guts looked like. I haven't seen Reger but he's alive, all right. Reger, he can take care of himself.*

I've only seen two of the aliens, or maybe I saw one of 'em twice. If you can imagine a horse-shoe crab made out of blue airfoam, a wide skirt all the way around it, the whole works about four and a half meters across, that's close. I'm not a biologist, so I guess I can't be much help on the details. That skirt sort of undulates front to back when it moves. I'd say it swims through the air—hop and glide, hop and glide. It can crawl too. First I thought it slid along like a snail but once I saw a whole mess of little legs, some with pincers on them. I don't know how many. Too many, anyhow. No eyes that I could spot, although it must have 'em; it's light in here, grayish, like on a snowfield on an overcast day. It comes from the bulkhead. Floor, too—everywhere.

Gravity, on a guess, is about one-sixth Earth. The atmosphere's hot. Seems to be light gases. I cracked my oxy relief valve and struck a spark on it with the back of my glove, and that was pretty spectacular. Hydrogen for sure. Something else that gives an orange cast to the flame. You figure it. I wish I knew as much as Reger. Though I wouldn't use it like he's doing.

The compartment I'm in is altogether bare. There's a transparent oval port on one bulkhead. No frame; looks just as if the hull material was made transparent just there. Looking in at an angle I can see she's double-hulled, and there's some sort of optical trickery that makes it possible to see almost directly forward and aft although I'd say the outside of the port was flush with the skin. I can't tell you a thing about the drive. I barely saw them before they had us boxed, and then all hell broke loose. I did get a look while we were adrift, though, and some of the ships were maneuvering. It isn't jets; that's for sure. They can take off like a bullet and stop as if they'd hit a wall. They have some way of cancelling inertia. Or most of it. Riding inside is pretty rough, but coming to a dead stop in two seconds from a thousand k.p.h. or better should butter you all over the walls instead of just slamming you into the bulkhead like it does. They can't operate in an atmosphere without wings, and they don't have wings. Yet.

I counted twenty-six ships—sixteen big ones, cruisers I guess you'd call them; two-fifty to three hundred meters long, perfect cylinders. And ten small ones, oblate spheres, thirty meters or so in diameter. Destroyers, maybe. Fast as hell, even compared to the big ones. I think my count's accurate, and you needn't expect any more than that. But that's plenty, with what they can do.

When they brought us in first they slung me in here and nothing happened that I knew about, for sixteen hours. Then that first bug came in through a sort of pucker in the wall that got transparent and spread out and let him through and then bing! the wall was solid again. I guess I was pretty paralyzed for a while, looking it over and then wondering which way it was going to jump. Then I saw what it was carrying on one side, the skirt-thing curled up like a sort of shelf. It was Minelli's leg lying there. That tattoo, you know, the girl holding the space-ship. I could see the top end of the femur, where it's supposed to fit into the hip-joint. That leg wasn't cut off. The joint had been torn apart.

I guess I went a little crazy. I had my antenna-wrench off the belt-rack and was throwing it almost before I knew what I was doing. I missed. Didn't allow for the gravity, I guess. It went high. The bug sort of humped itself and next thing I knew I couldn't move. I could, inside the space-suit, but the suit was like a single iron casting.

The bug slid over to me and hitched up a little—that's when I saw all those little legs—and got everything off my belt—torch, stillson, antenna-reel, everything that would move. It didn't touch my tanks—I guess it knew already about the tanks. From Reger, busy-boy Reger. It took the whole bundle over to the outer bulkhead and all of a sudden there was a square hole there. It dropped my stuff in and the hole went away, and out through the port I could see my stuff flash away from the ship, going like hell. So that's how I found out about the disposal chute.

The bug slid away to the other wall and I was going to give it a shot from my heel-jets, but somehow I had sense enough not to. I didn't know what damage they'd do, and I might be able to use 'em later. If anyone's reading this, I did.

Anyway, the bug went out, still carrying Minelli's leg, and when the wall went solid behind it I was free to move again.

About three weeks later I had another visit from one of 'em, but I charged it as soon as it was inside. It slid away through the air and then froze me again. I guess after that they gave me up as a bad job.

They don't feed me, and my converters are pretty low. I've rationed my air and water all I could, but it's past conversion now, without a complete recharge, and I'm not likely to get that. I was hungry, like I never knew hunger could be, after my emergency rations were gone, but I don't feel that any more. Just weak.

This whole time, the ships have been busy. We're in the Belt, I'd guess, without instruments, around 270-20-95. Check those coordinates and hunt a spiral from that center—I'm pretty sure we're near that position. Put infra-red on it; even if they've gone by then, there should be residual heat in these rocks out here. They've leeched onto a big one and it's practically gone now. They make long fast passes back and forth like a metal-planer. I can't see a ray or beam or anything, but the surface flows molten as the ships pass. Mining. I guess they filter the slag some way and distill the metals out. I wouldn't know. I'm a navigator. All I can think of is those ships making passes like that over the Golden Gate and Budapest and LaCrosse, Wisconsin.

I found out how to work the disposal chute. Just lean against it. It's an air-lock with some sort of heavy coils around it, inside, I guess to project refuse away from the ship so it won't orbit. They must've known I was fooling with it but nobody stopped me. They knew I couldn't get anywhere. Even if they knew about my heel-jets, they probably knew I couldn't get far enough with them to make no never mind.

Well, six hours ago a sort of dark spot began to show on the inboard bulkhead. It swelled up until it was a knob about the size of your two fists, shiny black, with some kind of distortion field around it so it was muzzy around the edges. For a while I couldn't figure it at all. I touched it and then took hold of it, and I realized it was vibrating around five hundred cycles, filling my suit with the note. I got my helmet onto it right away.

The note went on and then changed pitch some and

*finally spread out into a noise like a forty-cycle carrier, and
something started modulating it, and next thing it was saying my name, flat and raspy, no inflection. An artificial voice,
for sure. "Wain," it said, clearing itself up as it went along
"Wain, Wain."*

So I kept my head tight against it and yelled, "Wain here."

It was quiet for a while, just the carrier, and then the
voice came in again. I won't bother you with exactly what it
sounded like. The language was rugged but clear, like "Wain
we no have planet you have planet we take you help."

There was a lot of yelling back and forth until I got the
picture. And what I want to tell you most is this: once in a
while when I listened real carefully I heard another voice,
murmuring away. Reger—that I'll swear. It was as if this
voder, or voice machine, was being run by one of the bugs
and Reger was telling it what to say but they wouldn't trust
him to talk directly to me.

Anyway, the bugs had a planet and something had happened to it, I don't know what, but Earth was as close as
anything they'd seen to what they want. They figure to land
and establish a base and set up machinery to take over. They
had spores that would grow in our sea-water and get rid
of most of the oxygen, I guess by combining it with all the
elements in the ocean that could take it. Meanwhile they'd
convert rocks to put whatever else they needed into the atmosphere.

So damn cold-blooded . . . it wasn't us they were after.
You clear a patch of wood, you're not trying especially to
dispossess the squirrels and the termites. That just happens
while you work.

For a while I hoped we could maybe do something, but
item by item they knocked that out of my head. Reger'd told
'em everything. You look up that guy's record. He knows
atomics and ship design and chemistry and about every damn
thing, and it's all theirs. You know that field, or whatever,
that they paralyzed my suit with; its an application of the
inertia-control their ships have. You know, if you throw an
A-bomb at that field the bomb won't hit and it won't fire?
You couldn't even throw rocks at it—they'd have no inertia
at contact. They know we have no space fleet, only a half-
dozen exploring scouts, and the moon-shuttle.

We're done, that's all.

So I asked what's the proposition, and they said they could
use me. They didn't really need me, but they could use me.

They said I could have anything I wanted on Earth, and all the slaves I could put to work. Slaves. I heard Reger give 'em the word. I'd have thirty, forty years of that before they all died off. I'd work under Reger. He was directing the landing for them. Designing wings for them to come in on, too—that's what the mining was for, the wings. They'll put the base down in a desert somewhere, and first thing anyone knows the oxygen will start to go. And even if you do see 'em come in, you won't be able to touch 'em.

Maybe I shouldn't even try to warn you. Maybe it'll be better if you never know what hit you . . .

Reger, he . . . he's . . . ah, stick to facts, Wain. Something makes him hate Earth enough to . . . I don't see even a coward doing a thing like this just to save his skin. He has to have some other reason.

The bump on the wall said, "Reger says work with him, you can trust."

Yeah, I can trust. I told them what to do with their proposition and shove Reger along after it.

Now this is what I am going to do. Try, anyhow. My suit's the only one with a tape recorder, and it's internal. Could be that Reger doesn't even know about it. What I'm going to do is wait until this ship starts paring away at the asteroid. It gets up quite a hell of a speed at each pass, more than you'd think, because of the inertialess field. At the sunward end of one pass, I'll go out the chute. I'll have the ship's speed plus the throw-out coils in the chute.

I'll gyro around to head for the sun. I've wired the heel-jet starter to my oxy supply. When the oxy stops flowing the jets 'll cut in. I hope by then I'll be far enough away so they won't detect me, or won't bother with me. That's something I won't live to know about.

And I've wired the fuel gauge to my distress squealer. When the fuel's all gone the squealer'll cut in. There ought to be scouts out searching for my ship; maybe one will scoop me in.

We're positioning over the rock now.

Maybe I won't get through the chute. Maybe they'll powder me before I get clear. Maybe they'll pick up my jets when they cut in. Maybe they'll hear the squealer when the jets are gone. So many maybes.

Don't anybody call me a hero for doing this. I'm not doing it for you. I'm doing it to Reger. That bastard Reger . . .

Jerry Wain here, over and out.

*

The Major lifted his head from the report. Maybe one day he would be able to read it without his eyes stinging like this.

He lifted the flimsies away to uncover his own transcript. Coldly it listed the pertinent facts of his interview with the traitor's wife. He read them through again slowly, right through the last paragraph, which said:

SUMMATION: It is indicated that the subject is a brilliant but twisted individual, and that early influences as noted, plus his mode of life, have induced a morbid fear of himself and a deep distrust of every human being, including his wife. His extrapolative ability plus his vivid imagination seem to have created a certainty in him that he had been betrayed, or that he certainly would be. His actions as reported by Wain are apparently motivated by vengeance—a vengeance against all humanity including even himself.

The talker hissed, and a voice said, "Major, the Colonel would like your report on the Reger interview."

"Roger." He caught it up, held it, then slid it into his autowriter and rapidly tapped out:

The undersigned wishes to stress the partial nature of the above report, based as it is on the statement of a man under serious strain. Further evidence might conceivably alter the conclusions as stated.

He signed it and added his rank and section, rolled it, canned it and slapped it into the pneumatic tube.

"Now what the hell did I do that for?" he asked himself. He knew what the answer was. He rose and went to the mirror in the corner by the water-cooler, and peered into it. He shook his head in disgust.

*

When the ships were sighted, Wain's recording came out of the files and went straight to the wire services. One of the columnists said later that the ensuing roar from earth all but moved the moon out of its orbit. Suddenly there was no such thing as a secret weapon anywhere. Suddenly, there was—for the time being—nothing that could be called a nation. There was only the thunder of panic, fear, and fury, and in each of these, the name of Reger, rolling in the hollows of the Himalayas, blasting through the wide streets of

Buenos Aires and the alleys of London. They feared the alien, but they hated Reger.

Without Wain's recording, the alien might have slipped close, or even landed, before the world was alerted. Without it, a general alarm certainly would have awaited some sort of identification. But Earth was as ready as three billion fierce, fearing, furious humans could make it in the brief time they had.

The ships came single file, faster than any man-made object had ever travelled. They were exactly what Wain had described—sixteen large cylinders, ten small spheres. They were in six flights, one behind the other, each but one composed of both types, and the other an ominous line of five of the heavies.

They bore straight in for Earth, their single file presenting the smallest possible profile to Earth radar. (Reger knew radar.) When every known law of spatial ballistics dictated that with that course, at that velocity, they must plunge straight into the planet, they decelerated and swung to take up an orbit—rather, a powered course—around the planet, just out of rocket interceptor range (which Reger knew).

And now their wings could be seen. Telefax and television, newspapers and government agencies researched their contours in minutes. They were familiar enough—a gull-wing design which one aeronautical engineer described as having "every characteristic that could be built into a wing." Each wing, from root to tip, had its own reverse dihedral. Each was sharply tapered, and sharply swept back. Even the little spherical destroyers had them, along with a boom to support the butterfly tail. There was one Earth design almost exactly like it—an extremely stable large-plane airfoil for sub-sonic use. The designer: Wolf Reger.

The space scouts roared up to challenge them, heavy with armament and anger. They sent a cloud of missiles ahead of them. There was H.E. and atomics, solid-shot and a whole spectrum of random-frequency radio, just in case.

The radio waves affected the aliens precisely as much—as little—as the fusion warheads. Telescopic lenses watched the missiles race to their targets and simply stop there, to slide around the shining hulls and hang until, one by one, they were brought aboard.

And then the little scouts tried to ram, and were deflected like angling guppies from the sides of an aquarium, to go screaming off into space and a laborious turn.

For three days the enemy circled outside the atmosphere, holding their formation, absorbing or ignoring everything Earth could throw at them.

The Major telephoned Reger's wife to ask if she had removed her name from her mailbox and doorbell. She said indignantly that she had not, would not, and need not. The Major sighed and sent a squad down late that night to arrest her. She was furious. Yet she conceded his point fairly the next morning when she saw the newspaper photographs of her apartment. Even the window-frames were gone. The mob had chopped right through the floor in places, had even heaved the bathtub twelve floors down to the street. "You should know as much about people as you think you know about Wolf Reger," he said.

"You should know as much about Wolf as you do about people," she countered. There was, with her composure, a light he had not seen before. He said, suddenly, "You know something."

"I do?"

"You act as if you'd had a special delivery letter from that—from you husband."

"You're quite right."

"*What?*"

She laughed. It was the first time he had heard her laugh, and something with hands, ever so deep within him, wrung them.

"I shouldn't tease you, Major. If I promise to tell you when it's time, will you promise not to ask me now?"

"My job is to find out every little detail that can possibly bear on the situation," he said stiffly.

"Even if it didn't add one bit to your understanding?"

"You can't judge that."

"I certainly can."

He shook his head. "It's our job to decide. I'm afraid you'll have to tell me whatever it is."

Her gayety slipped away inside her, and a new kind of brightness shone in her eyes. "Well, I won't."

He began to speak, then stopped. He need make no experiments to discover that this extraordinary woman could not be bribed, coerced, or even surprised. He said gently, "Very well. I won't ask. And you'll tell me as soon as you can?"

"The very second."

He kept her in his office. She seemed not to mind. He let her read all the invasion reports as they came in, and he watched every flicker of expression in her face. "When are you going to admit that enough facts are in to show that there's no hero in this story, no one beating out flames?"

"Never. Have you ever been married, Major?"

Sourly, he thought, *Have you?* "No," he said.

"You've loved someone, though?"

He wondered how she kept her features so controlled under stress. He would like to learn that trick. He said, "Yes."

"Well, then. You only need a few facts about the one you love. Just enough to point the way."

"Three points on a graph to give you a curve, so you can know its characteristics and extend it. Is that what you mean?"

"That's one of the things I mean."

"They call that extrapolation. Your boy's specialty."

"I like that," she said softly. "I like that very much." She detached her eyes from him, from the room, and smiled at what she saw. "*God!*" he exploded.

"Major!"

"You're going to get clobbered," he said hoarsely. "You're going to get such a kick in the teeth . . . and there isn't a thing in the world I can do about it."

"Poor Major," she said, looking at him as if he were a memory.

There was a click, and electronic noise filled the room. The talker barked, "Enemy spiralling in. Stand by for trajectory."

"Now you'll see." They realized that they had spoken in unison, but it was the wrong time to exchange a smile.

"Arizona!" said the speaker, and "Stand by."

"Stand by hell," growled the Major. "We'll get the fine points by radio. Come on."

"You'll take me?"

"Wouldn't let you out of my sight."

They ran to the elevators, shot to the roof. A helicopter whisked them to the field, and a jet took them in and tore up and out to the lowering sun.

An unbroken cordon can be thrown about a hundred square miles in less than an hour and a half. This is true, because it was done immediately after the alien fleet touched Earth. Once the landing site was determined, the roads writhed with traffic, the desert crawled with men and machines, the air shook with aircraft, blossomed with parachutes. The ring had not quite closed when the formation came down almost exactly in the predicted center. No longer a single file, the formation was nearly spherical. It arrived on earth with two thunders—one, the terrible crack as the cloven air smashed back to heal itself, and rebounded and smashed again; the other, a shaking of the earth itself.

And the cordon stopped, flattened, lay still as a stain while the furious globe built itself in the desert, flung its coat of many colors about itself, mounted the sky and donned its roiling plumes.

And there were no devils there in the desert, but hell itself.

They saw it from the jet, because they were keeping close radio contact with the landing, and straining their eyes into the sunset for a glimpse of the fleet. Their pilot said he saw them, coming in at an impossible speed. The Major missed them as they blinked by, but he did see their wings, like a flurry of paper over a windy corner, drifting brokenly down. And then the fireball fought the sun and, for a while, defeated it, until it became a leaning ghost in a broad, torn hat.

It seemed a long, long time after that when the Major, his palms tight to his eyes, whispered, "You knew that would happen."

"No I didn't," she whispered back, cathedral-awed. "I knew something would happen."

"Reger did this?"

"Of course." She stirred, glanced at the tower of smoke, and shuddered. "Can you see yet?"

He tried. "Some . . ."

"Here," she said. "I promised you. My special-delivery letter."

He took it. "I've seen this. The picture of the fleet."

Exactly as she had once before, she murmured, "Poor Major." She took the print from him, turned it over, deftly slipped his gold pencil from under the pocket-flap of his tunic. "First there was a cruiser, and a cruiser, and a cruiser," she said, and drew a short line for each, one after the other, "and a destroyer and a destroyer." For each of these she made a black disk. "Then the second flight: destroyer, cruiser, destroyer." And so she charted the entire formation. He stared at the marks until she laughed at him. "Captain!"

"Yes ma'am," answered the pilot.

"Would you read this to the Major, please?"

She handed it forward. The Major said, "What do you mean, read it?" but she shushed him.

The pilot glanced at it and handed it back. "It says eighty-eight, thirty, W R."

"No, no—say the codes too."

"Oh—sorry." He glanced at it again. "It says 'Love and kisses. That's all I have for you. W R.' "

"Give me that," snapped the Major. "By God, it's morse!"

"He hung it up there for three whole days and you couldn't read it."

"Why wouldn't you tell me?"

"How would you have read it before *that* happened?"

He followed her gesture and saw the great hot cloud. "You're right," he breathed. "You're so right. He did that just for you?"

"For you. For everyone. It must have been the only thing he could do to let us know what he was doing. They wouldn't let him radio. They wouldn't even let him talk to Wain."

"Yet they let him deploy their ships."

"I guess because he made the wings for them; they thought he would know best how to use them."

"The wings tore off." To the pilot he said, "Isn't that what happened, Captain?"

"It sure is," said the young man. "And no wonder, the way they flashed in. I've seen that happen before. You can fly under the speed of sound or over it, but you better not stay just *at* it. Looked to me as if they hung on the barrier all the way in."

"All flown from one set of controls . . . probably an automatic pilot, with the course and speed all set up." He looked at the woman. "Reger set it up." Suddenly he shook his head impatiently. "Oh *no!* They wouldn't have let him get away with it."

"Why not?" she said. "Everything else he told them was true."

"Yes, but they'd have known about the barrier. Captain, just what is the speed of sound up in the stratosphere?"

"Depends, sir. At sea level it's around three-forty meters per second. Up at thirty kilometers or so it's around three hundred, depending on the temperature."

"The density."

"No sir. Most people think that, but it isn't so. The higher the temperature, the higher the speed of sound. Anyway, the 'sound barrier' they talk about is just a convenient term. It happens that shock waves form around a ship anywhere from eighty-five percent to one-hundred-fifteen per cent of the speed of sound, because some airflow around it is supersonic and some still subsonic, and you get real weird flow patterns. Some of the buffeting's from that, but most of it's from shockwaves, like the ones from the nose hitting the wing tips, or wing shock-waves hitting the tail."

"I see. Captain, could you set up a flight-plan which would keep an aircraft at the buffeting stage from the top of the atmosphere down to the bottom?"

"Imagine I could, sir. Though you wouldn't get much buffeting above 35 kilometers or so. No matter what the sonic speed, the air's too thin for shock wave formation."

"Tell you what. You work out a plan like that. Then radio Radar at Prescott and get the dope on Reger's approach."

"Yes sir." The young man went to work at his chart table.

"It's so *hard* for you," Mrs. Reger said.

"What is?"

"You won't believe it until your little graph's all plotted, with every fact and figure in place. Me, I *know*. I've known all along. It's so easy."

"Hating is easy too," said the Major. "You've probably never done much of that. But *un*hating's a pretty involved process. There's no way of doing it but to learn the facts. The truth."

They were five minutes away from the mushroom when the Captain finished his calculations. "That's it, sir, that's what happened. It couldn't have been an accident. All the way down, under power, those ships stayed within four percent of sonic speed, and tore themselves to pieces. And here's something else. Radar says that from 32 kilometers on down they showed a different pip. As if they'd shut off that inertia field of theirs."

"They'd have to, or they wouldn't have any kind of supporting airflow over the wings! You can't use an airfoil if the air can't touch it! I guess for some reason their inertia shield can't be used near a strong gravitic field."

"And Reger planned that approach, that way?"

"Looks like it. From thirty kilometers to the ground, at that speed . . . it was all over in fifteen seconds."

"Reger," muttered the pilot. He went back to the controls and switched off the automatics. "One of the radar pix showed Reger's space-suit, Major," he said. "Looks like he bailed out same as Wain did—through the disposal chute."

"He's alive!"

"Depends." The young man looked up at the Major. "You think that mob down there is going to wait while we compute velocities for 'em?"

"That's a military setup, Captain. They'll do what they're told."

"About *Reger*, sir?"

He turned his attention to the controls, and the Major went thoughtfully back to his seat. As they whistled down to the airstrip behind the cordon, he suddenly thumped his knee. "Light gases, high temperature—of *course* those bugs never heard of a shock-wave at what we call sonic speed! You see? You see?"

"No," she said. He understood that she did not need to see. She knew.

Maybe, he thought, the female of the species extrapolates without realizing it, and intuitive faith is nothing more than high-velocity computation.

He kept the thought to himself.

The Major walked quietly through the mob, listening. There were soldiers and Air Force men, security officers and civilians. Behind him, the cordon, tightening, reducing the strip between themselves and the radioactive area. In the cordon, a human gateway: FBI, CIA, G-2, screening those inside. The Major listened.

"He's got to be inside somewhere."

"Don't worry, we'll get the —"

"Hey George, tell you what. We get our hands on him, let's keep our mouth shut. Army gets him, it's a trial and all kind of foofaraw. This bunch gets him, they'll tear him to pieces right *now*."

"So?"

"Too quick. You and me, one or two other guys from around here—"

"I hear you."

From somewhere back of the cordon, a tremendous huffing and puffing, and a casual, enormous voice, "Mike hot, Lieutenant," and then the Psycho Warfare officer: "All right, Reger. We know you didn't mean it. No one here will hurt you. You'll get fair treatment all down the line. We understand why you did it. You'll be safe. We'll take care of you. Just step right up." And an interruption and a "Oh, sorry, Sir," and, clearly through the amplifier, "You don't coddle a son of a bitch like that while I'm around." Then, harshly,

Reger, step the hell up here and take your medicine. You
ot it coming to you and you're going to get it sooner or
ater."

The Major heard part of a suggestion about an operation
vith a blunt nailfile, and walked away from it into "You
ail one loop of gut to a tree, see, and walk him around it
ntil—"

The space-suit hung grotesquely by its neck against a shat-
ered barn wall. A scraggly man in filthy coveralls stood by
pile of rocks and chunks of four-by-four. "Just three for a
ime, gents, and the ladies free. Step right up and clobber
he son. Limber up for the real thing. I thank you sir: Hit
im hard." A corporal hefted a round stone and let fly. It hit
he space-suit in the groin and the crowd roared. The
craggly man chittered, "One on the house, one on the house!"
nd handed over another stone.

The Major touched a smooth-faced lieutenant on the arm.
What goes on?"

"Huh? The suit, sir? Oh, it's all right. G-2's been and gone.
His, all right. He's got to be around some place. Well, it's
is or the hot stuff—he can take his choice. The cordon's
getting radiation armor."

"There'll be hell to pay over this caper."

"Don't think so," said the lieutenant. "General Storms him-
elf pegged a couple."

"Make 'im bleed, corp'ral," shouted the barker to a pfc.
He hopped from one foot to another, jingling coins in his
ocket. "Whatsa matter, boys, you love 'im?"

"Imagine him, making a buck," said the Lieutenant ad-
niringly. "Regular clown."

"Yeah, a clown," said the Major, and walked away.

A soft voice said, "One look around here, I wish Reger'd
gotten away with it."

The Major said warmly, "You're a regular freak around
here, mister," and was completely misunderstood. The man
an away, and the Major could have bitten his tongue in
wo.

I want to be in a place, the Major thought suddenly,
passionately, *where the truth makes a difference.* And *If I
were a genius at extrapolation, where would I hide?*

"Mr. Reger, you're a reasonable man," bellowed the
speaker.

"Three for a dime. For a quarter you can throw a second
ootenant."

"He should hold out. He should go back into the bald-spot and fry slowly."

The cordon moved in a foot. *I just thought of the funniest gag*, thought the Major. *You pour vinegar on this sponge, see, and hold it up on this stick . . .*

Slowly he walked back toward the cordon, and then like a warm, growing light, it came to him what he would do if he were a genius at extrapolation, trapped between the advancing wolves and the leaping flames. He'd be a flame, or a wolf. But he couldn't be this kind of a flame. He couldn't be an advancing wolf. He'd have to be a wolf which stayed in one spot and let the advance pass him.

He went and stood by the man. This wasn't the notorious Reger face, hollowed, slender, with the arched nose.

He realized abruptly that the man's nose was broken and not bruised. And a man would have to wear coveralls for weeks to get them that filthy.

"I'll take three," he said, and handed the man a dime.

"Atta boy, Maje." He handed over two rocks and a billet. The Major aimed carefully, and said from the side of his mouth, "Okay, love-and-kisses. We've got to get you out of here."

The barker had an instant of utter stillness. Behind him, the speaker roared, "You can trust *me*, Mr. Reger."

The barker roared back, "An' I'll trust *you* Mr. Reger. Step right up and I'll let you have a coupla rocks." To the Major he said, "See, Maje? I'm in a position I can trust practically anyone."

The Major hurled his rock at the space-suit. From the side of his mouth, hardly moving his lips, he said, "High temperature, light gases, no barrier. I know what you did. Let me get you out of here." He threw again and hit the front of the space-suit.

"One on the house, one on the house. I like the way you're going, Maje."

The Major said, softly, "One thing you never extrapolated, genius. Suppose she loved you so much she would take you on faith when three billion people hated your guts?" He hurled the billet, and took out another dime. "I'll call it. I'm going to break a nose." He aimed slowly and said almost into his shoulder, "She never broke faith for a second. She's here now. Will you come?" He threw the rock and hit the face-plate.

"Come on, Reger," shouted the barker. "You got it coming to you sooner or later anyway." He picked up one of his

ocks, and whispered—whimpered, perhaps, "I might kill her
I go back . . ."

"She might die if you don't."

"There's one you never expected, Reger!" roared the barker,
nd threw his rock. "Want to yell a while?" he said to a
uck-toothed youth in overalls. "I got to go brush my teeth."
He walked straight toward the ambulant gate in the cordon,
he Major right behind him. Roughly, the Major shoved the
ttle man through. "If it's all the same to you," he said to the
BI man, "I'm curtailing this enterprise."

A CIA man nearby hitched at a shoulder holster and
rowled, "Fine idea, Major. I was about to mistake him for
eger, the dirty little bloodsucker." They passed outside.

"Never thought I'd find you yelling and gabbing and mixing
ke that," said the Major.

"You do what you have to do," said the little man. "I once
aw a woman lift a six-hundred-pound garage door with one
and and pull her little boy out with the other." He stumbled.

The Major caught him. "Man—you're whipped!"

"You don't know," he whispered. Suddenly, "Don't you
ove her enough to turn me over to *them?* You'll never
ave a better chance."

"Did I say I loved her?"

"One way or another."

They were quiet all the way back to the airstrip. The
Major said, in a choked voice, "I love her more than that
. . . enough to . . ." He thumped the side of the plane. "I
ound him," he called.

The door opened. "I knew you would," she said. They
elped Reger in. The Major climbed in beside the pilot.
Fly," he said.

The Major thought, *She knew I would. She has faith in me,
oo.*

A long time later he thought, *That's something, anyway.*

*Into the strange cosmos of Golden Age science fiction—
where first the plural of 'fans' was 'fen' and a letters' section
in the magazine became a 'lettercol' and the activities of fen
were 'fanac', and a fugghead was a 'fugghead'—came Samuel
Mines, from whence, fen never knew and, after a few issues
to where, few found out. Once a rumor passed briefly about
that Sam had died, eliciting a wail of anguish by long-dis-
tance phone from as far away as Peoria. However, I hold
here in my hand at this writing a letter from Sam Mines
who, like Mark Twain, calls the report 'exaggerated'—and I
am much pleased, for this man has been much loved. He
handled the 'lettercol' with extraordinary skill and com-
passion, and a good deal of quiet wit to boot. He engendered
some of the best letters the magazines ever ran; and those
magazines (Startling Stories and Thrilling Wonder) ran 'let-
tercols' the likes of which have never been seen before or
since. Sam happens, as well, to be a very good writer indeed
and one day someone in the general vicinity of the Pulitzer
Awards will be made aware of it.*

The Wages of Synergy

IT WAS the way they were breathing, she thought in despair
and disgust, that was making her mind run on like this. The
breathing was open throated in the darkness, consciously
quiet though its intensity was almost beyond control. It was
quiet because of the thin walls in this awful place, quiet to
hide what should have been open and joyful. And as the blind
compulsion for openness and joy rose, so rose the necessity
for more control, more quiet. And then it was impossible to
let her mind rest and ride, to bring in that rare ecstatic sun-
burst. The walls were growing thinner and thinner, surely
—and outside people clustered, listening. More and more people, her mind told her madly. People with more and more
ears, until she and Karl were trying to be quiet and secret
in the center of a hollow sphere of great attentive ears, a
mosaic of lobes and folds and inky orifices, all set together
like fish scales. . . .

Then the catch in his breath, the feeling of welcome, of gratitude . . . the wrong gratitude, the wrong relief, for it was based only on the fact that now it was over—but oh, be quiet.

The heaviness now, the stillness . . . quiet. Real quiet, this now, and no pretense. She waited.

Anger flicked at her. Enough is enough. This weight, this stillness . . .

Too much weight. Too much stillness . . .

"Karl." She moved.

"Karl!" She struggled, but quietly.

Then she knew why he was so quiet and so still. She looked numbly at the simple fact, and for a long moment she breathed no more than he did, and that was not at all, for he was dead. And then the horror. And then the humiliation.

Her impulse to scream died as abruptly as he had died, but the sheer muscular spasm of it flung her away from him and out into the room. She stood cowering away from the cold, the rhythmic flare of an illuminated sign somewhere outside, and again she opened her throat so her gulping breath would be silent.

She had to escape, and every living cell in her cried for shrieking flight. But no; somehow she had to get dressed. Somehow she had to let herself out, travel through corridors where the slightest glimpse of her would cause an alarm. There were lights, and a great glaring acreage of lobby to be crossed. . . .

And somehow she did all these things, and got away into the blessed, noisy, uncaring city streets.

Killilea sat at yet another bar, holding still another gin and water, wondering if this were going to be another of those nights.

Probably. When you're looking for someone, and you won't go to the police, and you know it's no use to advertise in the papers because she never reads the papers, and you don't know anyone who might know where she is, but you do know that if she is upset enough, unhappy enough, she drinks in bars—why then, you go to bars. You go to good ones and dirty ones, empty and bright and dusty and dark ones, night after night, never knowing if she's going to pieces in the one you went to last night, or if she'll be here tomorrow when you are somewhere else.

Someone sneezed explosively, and Killilea, whose nerves had always been good and who was, besides, about as detached from his immediate surroundings as a man can get, astonished himself by leaping off the bar stool. His drink went *pleup* and shot a little tongue of gin upwards, to lick the side of his neck coldly. He swore and wiped it with the back of his hand, and turned to look at the source of that monstrous human explosion.

He saw a tall young man with bright red ears and what had doubtless been a display handkerchief, with which he was scrubbing at the camel's hair sleeve of a girl in the booth opposite. Killilea's nostrils distended in mild disgust, while his lips spread in amusement just as mild. Sort of thing that might happen to anybody, he thought, but my God, that fellow must feel like a goon. And look at the guy in the booth with the girl. Doesn't know what to say. So what do you say? Don't spit on my chick? Too late. I'm going to punch you in the mouth? That wouldn't help. But if he doesn't do something he can't expect his lady-friend to be happy about it.

Killilea ordered another drink and glanced back to the booth. The tall young man was backing off in a veritable cloud of apologies; the girl was dabbing at her sleeve with a paper napkin, and her friend still sat speechless. He pulled his own handkerchief out, then put it back. He leaned forward to speak, said nothing, straightened up again, miserably.

"Fine Sir Galahad you turned out to be," said the girl.

"I don't think Galahad was ever faced with just this situation," her escort replied reasonably. "I'm sorry. . . ."

"You're sorry," said the girl. "That helps a lot, don't it?"

"I'm sorry," the man said again. Then slightly annoyed, "What did you expect me to do? Sneeze right back at him?"

She curled her lip. "That would've been better than just doing nothing. Nothing, that's you—*nothing.*"

"Look," he said, half rising.

"Going some place?" she asked nastily. "Go on then. I can get along. Beat it."

"I'll take you home," he said.

"Not me you won't."

"Okay," he said. He got out of the booth and looked at her, licking his lips unhappily. "Okay, then," he said. He dropped a dollar bill on the table and walked toward the door. She looked after him, her lower lip protruding wet and sulky. "Thanks for the neighborhood movie," she yelled at him, in a voice that carried all over the room. His shoulders gave a tight, embarrassed shrug. He grasped his lapels and gave his jacket a pathetic, angry little tug downward and left without looking back.

Killilea swung back to the bar and found he could see the booth in the mirror. "Big deal," said the girl, speaking into her open compact as if it were a telephone.

The tall young man who had sneezed approached cautiously. "Miss—"

She looked up at him calculatingly.

"Miss, I couldn't help hearing, and it was really my fault."

"No it wasn't," she said. "Forget it! He didn't mean nothing to me anyway."

"You're real nice about it anyway," said the young man. "I wish I could do something."

She looked at his face, his clothes. "Sit down," she said.

"Waiter!" he said, and sat down.

Now Killilea looked into his drink and smiled. Smiles didn't come easily these days and he welcomed them. He thought about the couple behind him. Suppose they had a great romance now. Suppose they got married and lived for years and years until they were old, and held hands on their golden wedding anniversary, and thought back to this night, this meeting: "First time you saw me, you spit on me. . . ." First time he saw Prue, she'd barged in on him in a men's room. Crazy, crazy, the way things happen.

"The way things happen," said a voice. "Crazy."

"What?" Killilea demanded, startled. He turned to look at the man next to him. He was a small man with pugnacious eyebrows and mild eyes, which became troubled and shy at Killilea's barking tone. He thumbed over his shoulder and said placatingly, "Them."

"Yeah," said Killilea. "I was just thinking the same thing."

The mild eyes looked comforted. The man said, "Crazy."

The door opened. Someone came in. It wasn't Prue. Killilea turned back to the bar.

"Waitin' for somebody?" said his neighbor.

"Yes," said Killilea.

"I'll beat it if your company gets here," said the man with the mild eyes. He breathed deeply, as if about to perform something brave. "Okay if I talk to you in the meantime?"

"Oh hell yes," said Killilea.

"Man needs somebody to talk to," said his neighbor. There was a taut silence as they both strove to find something to talk about, now that the amenities had been satisfied. Suddenly the man said, "Hartog."

"What?" said Killilea. "Oh. Killilea." They shook hands gravely. Killilea grunted, looked down at his hand. It was bleeding from a small cut in the palm. "Now how the hell did I do that?"

"Let me see," said the man called Hartog. "Oh, I say . . . I don't know what to . . . I think it was my fault." He showed his right hand, on the middle finger of which was a huge, gaudily designed ring with the gold plate wearing off the corners of the mounting. The stone was gone, and one of the mounting claws pointed up, sharp and gleaming. "I lost the stone yesterday," said Hartog. "I shouldn't have worn it. Turned it around inside my hand like always when I come to a place like this. But what can I do?" He looked as if he were about to cry. He worried at the ring until he could get it off, and dropped it into his pocket. "I just don't know what to say!"

"Hey, you didn't cut my arm off, you know," Killilea said good-naturedly. "Don't say anything. Not to me." Killilea pointed at the bartender. "Tell him what you're drinking."

They sipped companionably while the couple behind them laughed and murmured, while the jukebox unwound identical sentiments in assorted keys. "I fix refrigerators," said Hartog.

"Chemist," said Killilea.

"You don't say. Mix prescriptions, and all?"

"That's a pharmacist," said Killilea. He was going to say more, but decided against it. He was going to say that he was a biological chemist specializing in partial synthesis, and that he'd developed one he wished he could forget about, and that it had been so fascinating that Prue had left him, and that that had made him leave chemistry to look for her. But it would have been tiring to go through it all, and he was not used to unburdening himself to people. Even so, as Hartog had said, a man needs someone to talk to. I need Prue to talk to, he thought. I need Prue, oh God, but I do. He said, abruptly, "You're English."

"I was once," said Hartog. "How'd you know?"

"They call a drug store a chemist shop."

"I forgot," said Hartog; and this time, strangely, he seemed to be talking to himself, chidingly. Without understanding, Killilea said, "That's all right."

Hartog said, "I wonder if I spit on some girl she'll pick me up."

"It takes all kinds," said Killilea.

"*All* kinds," said Hartog, and nodded sagely. "All want the same thing. Each one wants to get it a different way.

Hell of a thing to know what one wants, not know how she wants it."

"Keeps it interesting," said Killilea.

Hartog fumbled a cigarette out of a pack without removing the pack from his pocket. "One been hanging out at Roby's, where I just was. You just *know* it about her, way she looks at everyone, way she watches." Killilea gave him matches. Hartog used one, blew it out with smoke from his nostrils, and stared for a long time at the charred end. "Funny little thing. Skinny. Everything wrong—bony here, flat there, and she got a big nose. Looks hungry. When you look at her you feel hungry too." He looked at Killilea swiftly, as if Killilea might be laughing at him. Killilea was not. "You feel hungry, not for food, see what I mean?"

Killilea nodded.

Hartog said, "I couldn't make it with her. Everything fine until you make *this* much—" he held a thumb and forefinger perhaps a sixteenth of an inch apart—"of a pass. Then she scares."

"A come-on."

"Nup," said Hartog. He closed his eyes to look at something behind them, and shook his head positively. "I mean scared—*real* scared. Show her a snake, shoot off a gun, she wouldn't scare like that." He shrugged. He picked up his glass, saw it was empty, and put it down again. Killilea was aware that it was Hartog's turn to buy. Then he noticed how carefully Hartog was keeping his eyes off Killilea's glass, which was also empty, and he remembered the way the single cigarette had come out. He beckoned the bartender, and Hartog thanked him. "Get up a parade," said Hartog. "Guys with ways to get a woman. Send 'em in one at a time to this funny little thing I'm telling you about. One brings sweet talk. One brings beads 'n' bracelets. One brings troubles to get sympathy. One brings sympathy for her troubles. One brings a fishtail Cadillac an' a four-carat blinker. One brings a hairy chest. All they going to do, all the specialists, they going to scare her, they won't get next to her a-*tall*."

"She doesn't want it then."

"You wouldn't say that, you see her," said Hartog, shaking his head. "Must be some way, some one way. I got a theory, there's a way to get to anything, you can only think of it."

Killilea swirled his drink. Bars are full of philosophers. But just now he wasn't collecting philosophers. "You selling something?" he asked nastily.

"I'm in the refrigerator repair business," said Hartog, apparently unaware of the insult. His ash dropped on his coat, whereupon he tapped his cigarette uselessly on the rim of an ashtray. "And why I keep talking about her, I don't know. Skinny, like I said. Her nose is big."

"All right, you're not selling," said Killilea contritely.

"Got only one ear lobe," said Hartog. "Saw when she pushed her hair back to scratch her neck. What's the matter, Mr. Killdeer?"

"Killilea," said Killilea hoarsely. "Which ear?"

Hartog closed his eyes. "Right one."

"The right one has a lobe, or the right one hasn't?"

"Taken in parts," said Hartog, "that's a real homely woman. Taken altogether, I don't know why she makes a man feel like that, but damn if she—"

Should I explain to this disyllabic solon, thought Killilea, that the day I met Prue in the men's room she charged out and went face-first through the frosted-glass door and lost an earlobe? And that therefore I would like very much to know if this . . . what had the idiot said? He'd just come from . . . Roark's . . . ? Rory's? *Roby's!*

Killilea turned and bucketed out.

The bartender blinked as the door crashed open, and then his cold professional gaze swung to Hartog. He advanced. Hartog sipped, licked his lips, sipped again, and put the empty glass down. He met the bartender's eye.

"Your friend forget something?"

Hartog pulled a roll of bills from a jacket pocket, separated a twenty, and dropped it on the bar. "Not a thing. Take it out of this. Build me another. Have one yourself and keep the change." He leaned forward suddenly, and for the first time spoke in a broad Oxford accent. "You know, old chap, I'm extraordinarily pleased with myself."

She didn't see him when he came into Roby's, which wasn't surprising. He remembered how she used to lean close to see his expression when they held hands. The only reason she had been in the men's room the day they met—what was it, four years ago? Five?—was that LADIES is a longer word than MEN, but the sign on this particular one said GENTLEMEN, and since it seemed to have more letters, she headed for it. She had glasses, good ones, but she wouldn't wear them, not without drawing the blinds first.

He moved to a table fifteen feet from hers and sat down. She was facing him almost directly, wearing the old, impenetrable, inturning expression he used to call her fogbound look. He had seen that face that way in happiness and in fright, in calm rumination and in moments of confusion; it was an expression to be read only in context. So he looked at the hands he knew so well, and saw that the left was flat on the table and the right palm upon it, pressing it from wrist to knuckles, over and over in a forceful sliding motion that would leave the back of the right hand hot and red and tender.

That's all I need to know, he said to himself, and rose and went to her. He put his big hand gently down on hers and said "It's going to be all right, Prue."

He pulled a chair close to her and silently patted her shoulder while she cried. When a waiter came near he waved the man away. In due time, he said, "Come home, Prue."

Her strange face whipped up, close to his. It was flogged, flayed, scored with the cicatrices of sheer terror. He had her hands and gripped them tightly as she started to rise. She sank down limply, and again she had the fogbound face. "Oh no, Killy; no. Never. Hear me, Killy? Never."

There was only one thing to say "—why?"—and since he knew that if he said nothing, she must answer the question, he was quiet, waiting.

Prue, Prue . . . in his mind he paraphrased the odd fantasy of Hartog, the barfly he had met this evening: Get up a parade. Ask the specialists, one by one, what do you think of a girl like Prue? (Correction: what do you think of Prue? There were no girls *like* Prue.) Send in a permanent secretary of the Ladies Auxiliary: *Sniff!* Send in a social worker: *Tsk!* A Broadwayite: *Mmm* . . . A roué: *Ah* . . . ! The definition for Prue, like beauty, could be found only in the eye of the beholder. Killilea had one, a good one. For Killilea —perhaps because he was a steroid chemist and familiar with complex and subtle matters—saw things from altitudes and in directions which were not usual. Prue lived in ways which, in aggregate, are called sophistication; but Killilea had learned that the only true sophistication lies in exemplary and orthodox behavior. It takes a wise, careful and deeply schooled gait to pace out the complicated and shifting patterns of civilized behavior. It takes a nimble and fleet hypocrisy to step from conflict to paradox among the rules of decency. A moral code is an obstinate anagram indeed. So Prue, thought Killilea, is an innocent.

And never to be with him again? Never? *Why?*

"It would kill you," she explained finally.

He laughed suddenly. "We understand each other better

than that, Prue. What awful thing has happened to me, then? Or what wonderful thing has happened to you?"

Then she told him about Karl. She told him all about it. "The men's floor of that silly hotel," she finished. "It seemed a sort of—different thing to do. We conspired . . . and it was funny."

"Getting out of there wasn't funny," he conjectured.

"No," she said.

"Poor Prue. I read about it in the papers."

"What? The papers?"

"About Karl's death, Miss Misty. Not about you! . . . He was quite an important man, you know."

"Was he?"

Killilea had long since ceased to be amazed at Prue's utter inability to be impressed by the things that impress everyone else. "He was a sort of columnist. More like an essayist. Most people read him for his political commentaries. Some people thought he was a poet. He shouldn't have died. We need people like him."

"He liked *The Little Prince* and mango chutney and he would rather look at penguins than baby rabbits," said Prue, stating her qualifications. "I killed him, don't you understand?"

"Prue, that's ridiculous. They had an autopsy and everything. It was heart failure."

She put her left hand flat on the table and with the right pressed and slid cruelly. "Prue," he said. She stopped.

"I did, Killy. I know I did."

"How do you know you did?"

That terror flitted across her face again.

"You can tell me, Prue."

"Because." She looked up into his face, leaning forward in that swift, endearing, myopic way. She so seldom really wanted to look at anything, he thought. The things she knows . . . the way she thinks . . . she doesn't *need* to see. "Killy, I couldn't bear it if you died. And you'd die."

He snorted. Gently, then, he asked her, "That isn't why you went away, is it?"

"No," she said without hesitation. "But it's why I stayed away."

He paused to digest that. "Why did you go away?"

"You weren't you any more."

"Who was I?"

"Someone who didn't look at the snow before it had footprints, someone who read very important papers all the way through the crêpes Suzettes, someone who didn't feed the goldfish," she said thoughtfully, and added, "Someone who didn't need me."

"Prue," he began, and cast about for words. He wished devoutly that he could talk to her in terms of ketoprogesterone and the eleventh oxygen in a four-ring synthesis. "Prue, I stumbled on something terribly important. Something that . . . you know those old horror stories, all built on the thesis that there are certain mysteries that man should not know? I always sneered at them. I don't any more. I was interested, and then fascinated, and then I was frightened, Prue."

"I know, Killy," she said. There was deep understanding in her voice. She seemed to be trying as hard as he was to find words. "It was important." The way she used the term included "serious" and "works of the world" and even "pompous."

"Don't you see, Killy," she said earnestly, "that you can have something important, or you can have me? But you can't have both."

There was a gallant protest to be made at this point, and he knew better than to make it. If he told her how very important she was, she would look at him in astonishment—not because she could not realize her importance to him, but because he would have so badly misused the term. He understood her completely. There was room in his life for Prue and his work when he built on his steroid nuclei as Bach built on a theme, surely and with joy. But when the work became "important," it excluded Prue and crêpes Suzettes and a lovingly bitten toe: music straight from a sunset rather than a sunset taken through music: the special sting across the sight from tears of happiness: and all the other brittle riches that give way when that which is "important" grows greater to a man than that which is vital. And she was perfectly right in saying that he had not needed her then.

"I've dropped it now," he said humbly. "All of it. No more fractionations. No more retained benzoquinones. No more laboratories, no more chemistry. Sometimes," he continued in her strange idiom, "there's a door to a flight of steps down to a long passageway, and it's magic every way you look. And on you go, down and around and along, until you find where it all leads, and that's a place as bad as a place can get. It's so bad you never want to go there again. It's so bad you never want the corridor again, or the steps. It's so bad you'll never go through the door. You close it and you lock it and you never even go near the door again."

"You wouldn't leave chemistry for me," she said factually.

"No, I wouldn't. I didn't. Prue, I'm trying to tell you that I closed the door eighteen months ago. Not for you. For me."

"Oh, Killy!" She was deeply concerned. "Not you! But whatever have you been doing instead?"

"Looking for you."

"Oh dear," she whispered.

"It's all right. All those fellowships, the prizes—I don't need chemistry any more. I don't even have to work. Prue, come with me. Come home."

She closed her eyes and her cheek bones seemed to rise toward them, so tightly were they sealed. She shook her head very slowly, twice, and at last a tear pressed through the lids. "I can't, Killy. Don't ask me, don't ever," she choked.

The inconceivable thought struck him, and the fact that it was inconceivable was the most eloquent thing which could be said about Prue and Killilea. "Don't you *want* to?" he asked painfully.

"Want to? You don't know, you can't. Oh, I want *so* much to." She made a swift, vague gesture which silenced him. "I can't, Killy. You'd *die*."

He thought about Karl and the dreadful thing that had happened to her. To call that experience traumatic would be fabulous understatement. But what peculiar twist made her insist that *he* might be harmed?

"Why are you so sure?" When he saw her face, he said, "You've got to tell me, Prue. I'll ask and ask until you do."

She leaned close to see his eyes. She looked into one, and the other. She touched his hair, a touch like the stirring of a warm wind. "Karl wasn't the first one. I . . . I killed Landey, Roger Landey."

Killilea's eyes widened. Landey, professor extraordinary, whose philosophy courses were booked solid two years in advance, whose deep wisdom and light touch had made legends before he was thirty . . . whose death four months earlier had shocked even the *Evening Graphic* into putting out a black-bordered edition.

"You *can't* really believe that you—"

"And someone else too. His name . . . they told me his name at a party." She wrinkled her brow and shook the wrinkles away impatiently. "I had a name for him that was much better. He was a round little man. He made you want to pick him up and give him a hug. I called him Koala.

I used to see him in the park. I gave him some leaves once, that's how I met him."

"Leaves?"

"Koalas look like teddy-bears and all they ever eat is eucalyptus leaves," she explained. "I saw him every day in the park and I began to wonder if he ever had any eucalyptus leaves, he reminded me so much of a Koala, I s'pose I thought he was one. I got some and went to him and gave them to him. He understood right away and laughed like . . . he laughed like you, Killy."

Killilea half-smiled through his distress, visualizing the scene; Prue so grave and silent, wordlessly handing the leaves to the man who looked like a koala . . . "Prue," he breathed. "Oh Prue . . ."

"I killed him too. The same way as the others, just the same. Here," she said suddenly. "Look, he gave me this." And from her pocketbook she drew a small cube and dropped it into his hand. It looked like blue glass, until he realized that it was not a cube but a chunk of monoclinic crystal.

"What is it?"

"It's lovely," was her typical answer. "Cup it in your hands, make it dark, and peek."

He put his hands together with the crystal inside, and brought it up to his eye. The crystal phosphoresced . . . no, he realized excitedly, it was fluorescing with a beautiful deep-blue glow, which had about it the odd "black-halo" characteristic of ultraviolet. But luminescents don't fluoresce without an energy source of some kind. Unless—"What is it?"

"You mean, what's it made of? I don't know. Isn't it just lovely?"

"Who . . . who was this Koala?" he asked faintly.

"Someone very fine," she said. Then she added, in a whisper, "That I killed."

"Don't say that ever again, Prue," he said harshly.

"All right. But it's true no matter what I say."

"What can I do?" he asked in despair. "How can I make you understand that these are crazy coincidences, that you had nothing to do with them?"

"Make me understand that I couldn't kill you, too, the same way. Can you do that?"

"Just take my word for it."

"No."

"Trust me. You used to trust me, Prue."

"You used to tell me things that were so. You used to say

things that came true. But if you'd begun to say this table is not a table, that lark isn't singing, it's a noise a cow makes . . . then I never could have trusted you at all."

"But—"

"Prove it to me, Killy. Find a way, I mean a real way, not words, not just clever ideas all strung out like a diamond necklace, all dazzly and going right around in a circle. Prove it a real way, like one of the things you did in chemistry. Build it, and show it to me. You can't show me I didn't kill those others, because I did. But show me I can't kill you, and I'll come . . . come home."

He looked at her for a long moment. Then he said, "I'll prove it to you."

"You won't ask me to come with you until you prove it?"

"I won't ask you," he said heavily.

"Oh, good, good," she said thankfully. "Because I can see you, if you'll promise that. I can see you and talk with you, Killy, I've missed you so very much."

They were together for a while longer. They let the waiter serve them. They exchanged addresses and left, and outside they parted.

Killilea thought, I had my work to keep me busy, and then I had Prue to look for. And I used to figure if I couldn't find her, I'd spend the rest of my life looking. If I could find her, I'd spend the rest of my life with her. I never thought what I might do if I found her and she wouldn't come home.

And here that's happened. But instead of a great big empty nothin'-to-do, I've got something to build.

Once I start. But where do I start?

Once home, he thought about that a great deal, while he smoked and paced. Part of the time he thought, this is no job for me. It's a psychopathologist's kick. And part of the time he thought, what can I do? I know I can do it, if I can only find the right thing to do. But I can't. And all this time he felt very bad. Then at last he thought about the one part of the problem you could pick up in your hand, look at, wonder about, find out. . . . The crystal.

He sprang to the phone, scrabbled through his number book, and dialed rapidly. The phone rang and rang at the other end, and Killilea was about to give up when a fast-asleep voice said "Hello," without a question mark.

"Hi. Egg?"

The voice came awake with a roar. "That's not Killilea?"

"Yup."

"Well godslemighty, where you been? What have you been doing for the last year? Hell, it's more than a year."

"Research," said Killilea, as the receiver made a yawning noise at him. "Gosh, Egmont, I just realized what time it is. I wake you?"

"Oh, that's all right. Like the man says, I had to get up to answer the phone anyway! What are you, up late or up early?"

"Egg, I'm racking my brains. Something I read some place, a crystal with a self-contained energy source that fluoresces."

"There's no such," said Egmont.

"Blue. Right up near the u-v.," persisted Killilea.

"Know anything about the lattice?"

"No. It's monoclinic, though."

"Hm. Nup—hey—wait! There is such a thing, but nobody ever gets to see one."

"No?"

"Not for a while yet. High-level blue, you say? I think what you're talking about is stilbene, crystallized after an infusion of tritium."

"Tritium!"

"Like I said, son. You won't find 'em on the toy counters this Christmas. Or next either, now that Pretorio checked out."

"Oh. Was that one of his tricks?" Killilea asked.

"His big trick," said Egmont. "Set up a whole line of constant light sources that way. Bid fair to do for crystallography what Jo-blocks did for the machine shop. Still a lot to do on it, though, and Pretorio was the boy could do it. Why, Killy? What's up?"

"Just got to worrying where I read about it. Egg, did you know Pretorio personally?"

"Had lunch with him one time. He was thirty-eight chairs due north of me. A convention banquet. Speaking of banquets *and* Pretorio, Killy, remember my offer to take you to the Ethical Science Board dinner one of these years?"

"Gosh yes! That'd be—"

"It wouldn't be," said the telephone. "I'm not going."

"I thought you were—"

"All het up about it? I was. I still am, about the main idea. But the outfit is but dead."

"I didn't know."

"What you expect?" barked Egmont. "Here's the finest idea of the century, see—to establish a genuine ethic for science, right across the board; to study the possible end effects on humanity of any progress in any science. They had Pretorio to run it, Landey the philosopher to steer it, and Karl Monck to correlate it with politics. And they're all dead. So where do you go when your car's suddenly missing a motor, the steering gear and a driver? I tell you, Killy, if some master-mind had set out to wreck the first real chance this crazy world ever had to get onto itself, he couldn't have done it more efficiently."

"But couldn't someone else—"

The wires sizzled. "Someone else!" Egmont inflected it like profanity. "Those three were unique, but not as unique as the fact that they were contemporaries. Where else are we going to find scientists who can buck the trend of anti-science?"

"Huh?"

"Yes, anti-science! Even the politicians are saying we have to turn to higher spiritual accomplishments *because* of what science has created. But their way of doing it will be to stop science from creating anything. It's a little like blaming the gunsmith every time somebody gets shot, but that's what's happening. Hell, four-fifths of the stories in science fiction magazines are anti-scientific." Egmont paused to breathe—at last—and said in more subdued tones, "Looka me. Off on a hobby horse, straight out of a sound sleep. Sorry, Killy. I'm lecturing."

"Gosh no," said Killilea. "Man's got something important to get excited about, he gets excited. Egg—"

"*Mmm?*"

"What did Pretorio look like?"

"Pretorio? Mild little guy. Pudgy." There was a pause while Egmont scanned a mental photograph. "He looked like one of those gentle little tree-climbing bears in Australia, know what I mean?"

"Koala," said Killilea.

"Something the matter Killy?"

God yes. "No, Egg . . . look, go back to bed. Swell talking to you again. I'll give you a buzz for lunch or a beer or something, sometime."

"Great," said Egmont. "Do that. Soon, huh? 'Night."

Slowly Killilea hung up and went to sit on the edge of his bed. He thought, I quit chemistry because I was about to isolate the most ghastly substance this earth has ever known, and I didn't want it isolated.

But I think someone has finished my work. . . .

Killilea, as anyone who met him could attest, was not an ordinary man. The ways in which he was extraordinary did not include fictional commonplaces like the easy familiarity with phones, cabs and the police methods of a private eye and the adventure-hero's fisty resourcefulness. He was a scientist—or rather, an ex-scientist—rather more sure of things he did not believe in than those in which he did. His personal habits tended toward those of a hermit, though intellectually he recognized no horizons. He was at a serious disadvantage with other people because of a deep conviction that people were good. And though he had found that most were good, the few who were not invariably caught him off-guard. His work in biochemistry had been esoteric in the extreme, and he had worked in it alone. But even if it had been more general an endeavor, he would not comfortably have worked with anyone else.

So now he found himself very much alone; no allies, no confidants. Yet he had always worked this way in the lab; you find a brick that fits a brick, and see what you can build with them. Or you know what to build, and you find the bricks that will do the job.

He called Prue late the next morning, and she was not at home. So he went back to the restaurant where he had found her, not expecting to see her, but simply because he felt he could think better there.

The table they had had was vacant. He sat down and ordered some lunch and a bottle of ale, and stared at the chair she had used. Somewhere, he thought, there is a lowest common denominator in all this. Somewhere the deaths of three great liberal scientists in Prue's arms, and the work I have been doing are tied together. Because what I almost had was a thing that would make men die that way. And since it was men it would work on, and not women, then Prue isn't the lowest common denominator.

Under the arch which separated the dining room from the bar a man stopped and gasped audibly. Killy looked up into the man's shocked face, then turned around to find out what had so jolted him. A wall, some tables—nothing else. Killy turned back again and now had time to recognize the man —the philosophic barfly, Hartog. "Hi."

Hartog came forward timidly. "Oh. Mr.—uh . . ."

"Killilea. You all right?"

Hartog hesitated, his hand on a chair. "I—I get a twinge now and again," he said. "I don't want to horn in."

"Sit down," said Killilea. The man looked badly shaken.

"Well," he said, and sat down. Killilea beckoned the waiter. "Had lunch?"

Hartog shook his head. Killilea ordered a double sirloin. "Medium rare all right?" and when Hartog agreed gratefully, sent the waiter off.

"Is your hand all right?" Hartog asked. "I'm real sorry about that."

Killilea noticed he had removed the ring. "I told you last night to forget it. Uh—while people are apologizing, I just remembered I belted out of that bar sort of suddenly last night. Did I pay or not?"

"Yes, it's all right," said the other. His fierce brows drew together. "I sort of had the idea you went after that funny little girl I was telling you about."

"You did?"

"Well, I don't want to pry," said Hartog mildly. "Just wondered how you made out, that's all."

Killilea let the subject lie unnoticed until it went away. He finished his ale and waved the bottle at the waiter.

"Women are trouble," Hartog mumbled.

"I heard," said Killilea.

"I like to know where I stand," Hartog said reflectively. "Like if I have a girl, I like to know is she my girl or not."

"When you say *your* girl," asked Killilea, "what do you mean?"

"Well, you know. She's not playing around."

"Do you talk about women all the time?" Killilea demanded with some irritation.

Hartog answered mildly, in his uninsulted way, "I guess I do. Does it make you mad, your girl two-timing you? I mean," he added quickly and apologetically, "say you have a girl and she does play around."

"It wouldn't happen," Killilea said bluntly. "Not to me."

"You mean any woman does that to you, you'll throw her out?"

"That's not what I mean," said Killilea. He pushed back a little and let the waiter set out the steak and the two bottles of ale.

"Fidelity," said Hartog. "What about fidelity? You don't think it's a good thing?"

"I think it's a bad thing," said Killilea.

"Oh," said Hartog.

"What's the matter?"

Hartog, in two senses, addressed his steak. With his

mouth full, he said, "I had you figured as a man would stick by a woman, whatever."

"You figured right."

"But you just said—"

"Look," said Killilea, "I don't know what the word 'fidelity' was supposed to mean when people first began to use it, but it's come to mean being faithful, not to a person, but to a set of regulations. It's a kind of obedience. A woman that brags about fidelity to her husband, or a man that's puffed up because he's faithful to his wife—these people are doing what one or two zebras, a few fleas, and millions of dogs do—obey. Point is, they have to be trained to do it. They have to develop a special set of muscles to stay obedient. It's a—a task. I think it's a bad thing."

"Yeah, but you—"

"Me," said Killilea. "If what I have with someone needs no extra set of muscles—if I don't and couldn't want anyone else—then I'll stick with it. Not because I'm obedient. But because I couldn't do anything else. I'd have to have the extra set of muscles to break away."

"Yeah," said Hartog, "but suppose your girl don't feel the same way?"

"Then we wouldn't have anything. See what I'm driving at? If you have to work at it, it isn't worth it."

"So when you don't have that kind of a life with someone, what do you do—play the field, I guess, huh?"

"No," said Killilea. "I have that kind of a life, or none at all."

"Sounds like a lazy man's way to me," said Hartog, the timidity of his eyes taking the sting out of the statement.

Killilea smiled again. "I said I wouldn't work at it," he said softly. "I didn't say I wouldn't work *for* it."

"So you wait for the one woman you can live like that with," said Hartog, "and unless you find that one, you pass 'em all up, and if you do find her, you pass up all the others. Right?"

"Right."

Hartog said, "Those regulations you talked about, don't they call for just that kind of living?"

"I suppose."

"Then what's the difference?"

"I guess," said Killilea, "it's in the way you feel when you do it because you want to and not because you're told to."

"Oh."

"You know, you sound downright disappointed."

Hartog met his eyes. "Do I? Well, maybe . . . I had a chick I thought maybe you should meet. You are alone, aren't you?"

"Yes," said Killilea, and thought of Prue with a pang. Then his eyes narrowed. "You were going on like this last night too. Are you *sure* you're in the refrigerator business?"

"Aw, don't get salty," said Hartog. "It's just I hate to see anybody lonesome when he don't have to be."

"You're very kind," said Killilea sourly. "I wish you hadn't gone to the trouble."

"Shucks," said Hartog. "You're mad. You shouldn't get mad. Just wanted to do what I could, and only found out it was wrong by doing it."

Killilea laughed, relenting.

"Killy. . . ."

He leapt to his feet. Prue had come in so quietly he had not seen her. But then, she always moved like that.

"Hello," said Hartog.

"I'll come back later," said Prue to Killilea.

With that, Hartog forked in a lump of steak as big as his two thumbs, and rose. "I got to go anyhow," he said slushily around it. He looked at Killilea, fumbled toward his pocket.

"Forget it," said Killilea. "I'll pick up the tab."

"Thanks," said Hartog. "Thanks a lot. So long."

"Good-by," said Killilea.

" 'By," said Hartog to Prue.

Prue turned to Killilea. "I hadn't hoped to see you so early today."

Hartog hesitated embarrassedly, then went out through the arch. "What's the matter, Prue?"

"I don't like him," she said in a low voice.

Killilea remembered, belatedly, Hartog's account of his fruitless efforts to get somewhere with the funny little girl with one ear lobe. He had a moment of fury, and quickly molded it into laughter by application of some objectivity.

"He's harmless," he said. "Forget him, Prue. Sit down. Have you had lunch?"

"I'd like an apple," she said. "And some toast."

He ordered them, deeply pleased in some strange way because it was unnecessary to suggest anything else to her. It was good to know her so well. Soft and strange and so very sure . . . Prue . . . he felt a surge of longing that almost blinded him, and he all but put out his arms hungrily to her. But with the impulse came the thought, I know so well that an apple and some toast is her lunch, the only lunch she wants; and I know just as well that she was just that sure when she said she wouldn't come home.

He took her hands and put his face close to hers so she could see how serious he was. "Prue, I need help. You'll help me, won't you, Prue?"

"Oh yes. . . ."

"I'll have to talk about 'important' things."

"I don't know if I can help with those," she half-smiled.

"I'll have to talk about chemistry."

"I won't understand."

"I'll have to talk about Koala and the others. . . ."

"Oh. . . ."

"You'll help me, won't you?"

"Killy, I'll try."

"Thank you, Prue."

"Why don't you ever call me 'darling' and 'sweetheart'?"

"Because 'Prue' means all those things and says them better."

Prue nodded gravely at his explanation, not flattered, not amused, having asked and received information. She waited.

"I have a lot of pieces, but not enough," he began. "I can put some together, but not enough. They make some sense, but not enough." He lifted his glass and stared at the fine lacework of foam that clung to the inside surface. With one finger he wiped away a little semicircle of it, and then another, until he had the words he needed.

"Chemistry is a strange country where sometimes the whole is greater than the sum of its parts, if you put the right parts on top. When one reaction finishes with *blue,* and another reaction finishes with *hot,* and you put the end products together and the result is bluer and hotter than the blue one and the hot one before, that's synergy."

"Synergy," Prue repeated dutifully.

"The thing that made me leave chemistry was something so fascinating that I followed it too far, and so complicated that it would take me most of the day to explain it to somebody who knew my branch as well as I do. It's up a broad highway and sharp left down a little road that no one knows is there, and across a sticky place to a pathway, and then out where no one's ever been before.

"That's an analogy, and so was what I was doing. I was trying to understand what happens chemically throughout the whole sexual process. That's an orchestration, you know, with more pieces in its music than any conductor ever used. There are subtle and tiny parts to be played by finely made and exquisitely measured chemicals—so much from the strings, so much from the brasses. And there are cues to be followed, so that the flutes are silent until they can pick up the theme the horns give them.

"And that's an analogy of an analogy, the music that sweeps on to its climax and is scored from beginning to end. But there are even chemical motifs that aren't scored, for they happen before the music and after it, in silence. In a man's head, nestled deep down below and between the halves of his brain, lies a little nubbin which has a strange and wonderful power, for it can take a thought, or the very shadow of a thought, and with it sound an A that can send the whole orchestra rustling and trembling, tuning up. And there are chemical workers who let the curtain down, send the musicians away to do other work—they're all very talented and can do many things—and pack away the chairs and music stands.

"In my chemical analogy I made a working model of that process; if the real thing was music, mine was poetry that strove to create the same feelings; if the real thing was the course of a hunting swallow, mine was the trajectory of a hungry stingray.

"I did it, and it worked, and I should have left it alone. Because through it I found a substance which did to the music what you do when you turn off your phono-amplifier. This substance killed, and it did it just at that great final resolving crescendo. I isolated it because it made the experiment fail and it had to be removed. The experiment then succeeded —but I had found this terrible substance. . . . I left chemistry."

His hands, twined together, crackled suddenly. She touched them to cool them. "Killy, that was just an analogy, though. It wouldn't work on a person."

He looked away from the hands to her face. "The analogy was too clear, too close. Anyone who understood it could follow it through, and apply it. You don't need a Manhattan project to make any but the first bomb. All you need after that is a factory. You don't need scientists—engineers will do. And when they're done with it, all you need is mechanics.

"Prue, Prue . . . it's synergy, you see? All the products of all the ductless glands, tempered and measured to build the climax, and then the tiny triggering, and the synergistic re-action flooding into the medulla, where a marvellous being lives, telling the heart when to beat, the lungs to expand, even instructing the microscopic fingers of the cilia which nudge the nutrients through the yards of digestive tract. The medulla simply stops, and everything stops. Yes, yes, heart failure," he almost sobbed.

"But Killy . . . you didn't make any of it!"

"No, I didn't. But I found out how, and I want no part of it."

"A dream," she said. "A horror. But—it's something in a museum. It can't get out. Poison in a locked cabinet—a guillotine in a picture-book—they can't get out to hurt people, Killy."

"You're my true Prue because you could never in a thousand years see how this could get out and hurt people," he said thickly. "Because you have your world and you live in it your way, and it doesn't touch this other, where three billions teem and plan and ferment evil. Let me tell you the ugly thing then." He wet his lips. "Do you know what would happen with this substance in a world where men can soberly plan the use of such a thing as an H-bomb? I'll tell you. It would be snatched up. It would be synthesized by the bucket, by the thousand-gallon tank. It would be sprayed out as a mist over human beings and their cities and their land. And then the ghastly thing that has happened to you three times already would happen to thousands, to millions of women. *Leibestod*—love-death."

Her face was chalky. "It *was* me, then. It's been done to me. . . ."

"No!" he roared. Heads turned all over the restaurant, and that was a blessing, because it brought him into the present where he had to remember appearances and modes and manners, and, remembering, relieve the awful pressure of what he was saying. "This synergy is purely a complex of male functions. The synergic factor would be absorbed painlessly and without warning, through the lungs, through any tiny break in the skin. Then it would lie in wait until just the proper impulse of just the mixture of hormones and enzymes, and all their fractions, set it free. And that is. . . ."

"*Liebestod*," she whispered.

"You still don't realize how devilish this is. Being you, you can't. You see, it would do more than kill men and put their women through the hell you already know. It would throw a city, a whole nation, a culture, into an unthinkable madness. You know the number of pitiful sicknesses that are traced to frustration. Who would dare to relieve frustration with a ghostly killer like that loose in the land? What of the conflicts within each man, once the thing was defined for him? (And defined it must be, because the people must be warned!) Do you know of the old psychology-class joke, 'Don't think of a white horse'? What else could a man afraid to be alone, he'd be afraid to read, he'd be afraid to sleep, he'd be afraid to be alone, and he'd be afraid to be with others. In a week there would be suicides and mutilations; in two they would start to murder their women to get them out of sight. And all the while no man would truly know whether the sleeping devil lay within him or not. He'd feel it stir and murmur whether it was there or not.

"And their women would watch this, and slowly understand it. And the little children would watch, and they would never understand it, and perhaps that is the worst thing of all.

"And this is my accomplishment."

Nothing, nothing at all could be said at that time. But she could be with him. She could sit there and let him know she was close, while he lost himself for a long moment in the terrible pictures that flashed and burned across the inner surface of his closed eyelids. . . .

At last he could see again. He tried to smile at her, the kind of tortured effort that a woman remembers all her life. "So you can come home with me," he said shakily.

"No, Killy."

All he did was to close his eyes again.

"Don't, Killy, please don't," she wept. "Listen to me. Understand me. You didn't make the factor—but someone has. You say there's no way of knowing whether it's within you or not. Well, it was there in three men who died, and it may be in you."

"And it may not," said Killilea hoarsely. "If not—good. And if it is—do you think I've wanted to live, this last year and a half?"

"It doesn't matter what you want!" she snapped. "Think of me. Think of me, think of yourself dying that way, with me . . . and each time might be the last, and it would all be a hell where every love-word was a threat. . . . No, Killy!"

"What, then? What else?"

"You have to stop it. There's got to be a way to stop it. You have a clue—Landey and Karl and Koala. Think, Killy! What had they in common?"

"You," he said cruelly.

Any other woman on earth would have killed him for that. But not Prue. She didn't even notice it, except as part of the subject in hand. "Yes," she said eagerly. "Why, then? Why me?"

"I wouldn't know that." Almost in spite of himself, his brain began to search, to piece, to discard and rematch. "They were all scientists. Well, not Karl Monck. I don't know—maybe he was a sort of thought-scientist. A human engineer."

"They were all—good." she said. "Gentle and thoughtful. They truly cared about people."

"They were all members of the Ethical Science Board. Pretorio founded it. It's going to die without them, too."

"What was it supposed to do?"

"Synthesize. Make people understand science—not what it is, but what it's for. Make scientists in one branch understand scientists in another—keep them working toward the same ends, with the same sense of responsibility. A wonderful thing, but there's no one left who has both science and ethics to such a degree that the Board can be anything but a social club."

Her eyes glowed. This was a thing she could really understand. "Killy, would anyone want to stop work like that?"

"Only a madman. Why, such a Board could—"

"I think I know what it could do. What kind of a madman, Killy?"

He thought about it. "Perhaps the old-time 'robber-baron' —the international munitions-maker, if he still existed, which he doesn't, since governments took over the munitions trade."

"Or someone who might try to sell it to the highest bidder?"

"I wouldn't think so, Prue. A man can get terribly twisted, but I can't believe a mind capable of reasoning a series of reactions as complex as this one could fail to see consequences. And one very likely consequence is the end of an environment where his riches would mean anything."

"Every pathway has a big 'No' sign," she murmured.

"That's what I've been living with," he said bitterly.

They were silent until Prue said, "They were all like you."

"What? Oh—those three . . . whatever do you mean, Prue? Karl with his deep socio-political insights, me with nothing but bewilderment in the everyday world. Landey, that philosophy of his . . . oh, Prue! He was a scholar and a humorist; that isn't me! And Pretorio, your koala—him and his EINAC brain! No, you couldn't be more wrong."

"I'm right," she said. "They were like you. I couldn't have been with them if they weren't."

"Thank you," he said ardently, "But how?"

"None of them were . . . pretty men," she said slowly. "They all respected homo sapiens, and themselves for being members of it, for all they feared it. They all feared it the way a good sailor fears a hurricane; they feared it competently. They all laughed the way you do, from deep down. And they all still knew how to wonder like children."

"I don't quite know what to say to that."

"You can believe me. You can believe *me*, Killy."

"I do, then; but that doesn't help." Again he plunged into thought, seeking, turning, testing. "There's only one single hypothesis so far. It's crazy. But—here goes. Someone was gunning for those three, maybe because of the Ethical Science Board. He discovered my fractionations and synthesis, maybe independently, maybe not. Maybe not," he repeated, and filed the question in his mental 'pending' folder.

"Anyway, he succeeds—I don't know how; he injects the factor into those three men without their knowing it; he divines that all three would find you deeply appealing; he sees to it that each in turn meets you. He must have kept a pretty close watch on things, all the time—" Prue shuddered—"and so he kills them."

Prue said, in a dead voice, "You can add to that." She took his hand. "There were not three, but four men he was after, and he wants you to take me back home. If that doesn't work he will try something else. Killy, be careful, careful!"

"Why?" he asked, and cracked his knuckles against the side of his head. "Why? What would anyone gain that way?"

"You said it yourself. It would cripple the Board, maybe kill it. Oh, and another thing! If he knows about the factor, how to make it, how to use it, he probably knows that you know it, too. He wouldn't want that, don't you see? He wouldn't want someone like you around, alert, watching for some sign of that hellish thing, ready to tell the authorities, the Government, the Board about it. He'd want that secret kept until it was too late to stop it.

"You'll have to find him and kill him."

"I'm not a killer," he said.

"There isn't any other way. I'll help you."

"There are always other ways." He was shocked.

"You're so . . . damn . . . wonderful," she said suddenly.

Again he was shocked. It was the first time he had ever heard her say "damn."

"I had a think," she said detachedly. The phrase thrilled the part of him that was always so nerve-alive to her; so many rich moments had begun with her sudden, "Killy, I had a think. . . ."

"Tell me your think," he said.

"It was after I went away," she said, "and I was alone, and I had the think, and you weren't there. I made a special promise to save it for you. Here is the think: There is a difference between morals and ethics, and I know what it is."

"Tell me your think," he said again.

"An act can be both moral and ethical. But under some circumstances a moral act can be counter to ethics, and an ethical act can be immoral."

"I'm with you so far," he said.

"Morals and ethics are survival urges, both of them. But look: an individual must survive within his group. The patterns of survival within the group are morals."

"Gotcha. And ethics?"

"Well, the group itself must survive, as a unit. The patterns of an individual within the group, toward the end of group survival, are ethics."

Cautiously, he said, "You'd better go on a bit."

"You'll see it in a minute. Now, morals can dictate a pattern to a man such that he survives within the group, but the group itself may have no survival value. For example, in some societies it is immoral *not* to eat human flesh. But to refrain from it would be ethical, because that would be toward group survival. See?"

"Hey." His eyes glowed. "You're pretty damn wonderful yourself. Lessee. It was 'moral' to kill Jews under Hitler, but unethical in terms of the survival of Humanity."

"It was even against the survival of Germany."

He looked at her in fond amazement. "Did you bring all this out because of what I said—I'm not a killer?"

"Partly," said Prue. "Even if I agreed that killing that hypothetical devil of ours was immoral—which I wouldn't—what about the ethics of it?"

He grinned. "Check, comma; mate. I'll kill him." The grin faded. "You said 'partly.' Why else do I get this study in pragmatism?"

"I'll tell you when you're uncluttered a bit. That is, if you don't think of it yourself first. Now then: how do we find him?"

"We might wait until he goes after me."

"Don't even think that way!" she said, paling.

"I'm serious. If that's the only way, then we'll do it. But I admit I'd rather think of another. Good gosh, Prue, he has an identity. He's been around, watching—he *must* have been. He's someone we know."

"Start with the fractionations. Did you keep notes that anyone might have seen?"

"Not after I began to suspect what I was getting to, and that was comparatively early. Up to that point it was fairly routine. I told you it went off into a side-road no one knew about."

"Could anyone have studied your apparatus—what was left in the stills and thingummies?"

"The stills and thingummies were cleaned enough and dismantled enough to bewilder anyone, every day when I was through with them," he said positively. "You do just so much classified and secret work and you get into habits like that. Of course, some of that apparatus was—no," he said, and shook his head. "It wouldn't tell anyone anything unless they knew the exact order in which the pieces were set up."

"You weren't a Board member at all," she mused.

"Me? I was a hermit—remember? Oh sure, I knew I'd join it some time. Matter of fact, I had a date for their banquet next month, which was cancelled. Fellow who was taking me is dropping out because of those deaths. Says the Board is dying or dead already." Prue seemed to be waiting for something, so he said "Why?" He thought he detected the smallest slump of disappointment in her shoulders.

"Could there have been anything the Board was about to do that would be undesirable or dangerous to anyone?"

"Now, that I wouldn't know." He scratched his ear. "I think I can find out, though. Hold on. Don't go away." He sprang to his feet, stopped, and turned back. "Prue," he said softly, "you're not going to go away again, are you?"

"Not now," she said, her eyes bright.

He went to the telephone, dropped in a coin and dialed Egmont's number. "Hello—Egg? Hiya. Killy here."

"What is it you want, Killilea?"

Killilea had already started to talk by the time he realized how formal and frigid Egmont's voice was. A small frown appeared, but he went right on. "Look, you were pretty much in on the Ethical Science Board doings until recently, weren't you?"

There was a pause. Then "Suppose I was?"

"Cut the rib, Egghead," said Killilea. "This is serious. What I want to find out is, do you know if Pretorio or Monck or Landey, singly or in combination, had anything up their sleeves before they were killed? Some bombshell, or very important announcement that they were about to spring at a meeting?"

"Whatever I know, Killilea, I most certainly am not passing on to you. I want to make that absolutely clear to you."

Killilea's jaw dropped. Like most men who genuinely liked people, he was extraordinarily vulnerable to this sort of thing. *"Egg!* he gasped, then, almost timidly, "This *is* Egmont . . . Richard Egmont?"

"This is Egmont, and I have no information for you, not now or ever."

Click!

Killilea walked slowly back to the table, rubbing his ear, which was still stinging.

Prue looked up, and started. "Killy! What happened?"

He told her. "Egg," he said. "Hell, I've known him for . . . what do you suppose is eating . . . why, I never—"

Prue patted his arm. "I hate it when something hurts you. Why didn't you ask him what was wrong?"

"I didn't have time," said Killilea miserably. "Hey!" he barked. "Somebody's been working on him. If we can find out who—"

"That's it, that's it," said Prue. "Call him again!"

Back in the booth, Killilea set his jaw and waited for the first sound of Egmont's voice. Being struck under his guard was one thing: going after something he urgently wanted was something else again.

"Hello?"

"Listen, you," growled Killilea. "Hang up on me and so help me I'll come over there to that office of yours, gag your secretary and kick your door down. The only way you can get rid of me is over the phone."

He could hear Egmont's furious breathing. Finally, "I don't care what you do, you're not getting any Board information out of me."

"Hold it!" snapped Killilea as he sensed the other receiver coming down. Egmont said "Well?"

"All I want to know is what's gotten into you since last night. You sound like I'd punched your grandmother, and I haven't even seen her."

"You're a pandering little scut," growled Egmont.

Killilea squeezed his eyes tight and bit back the rage that had begun to churn inside him. "Egmont," he said somberly, "we were friends for a long time. If you did something I didn't like I might write you off, but damn it I'd tell you why first. At least you owe me that. Come on—tell me what's with you. I honest-to-God don't know."

"All right," said Egmont, his voice shaking. "You asked

for it. I'm going to tell you a thing or two about your buddy that you don't know."

"Buddy? What buddy?"

"Just shut up and listen," hissed Egmont. "You make me madder every time you open your mouth. Jules Croy, that's what buddy. You and your bright and cheerful questions about the Board. This is the guy that's taking over what's left of the Board and making a marching and chowder society out of it—a damned jackal, a corpse-eater."

"But I don't—"

"More money than he knows what to do with, and nothing to do with his time but hatch up what's left of the finest damn. . . ." He subsided to a splutter, and then growled, "And you. Spying around, seeing what you can pick up. You're just right for it, too, the hermit with the big name in science, back in circulation again, picking up loose ends. Well, anybody I can get to won't have any ends to give you. You louse!"

"Now you hold it right there," flared Killilea. "That's damn well enough, Egmont. I've heard of this Croy—who hasn't? But I wouldn't know him if he was in this phone booth with me. I've never had a single damned word with him!"

Egmont's voice was suddenly all disdainful amazement. "If I didn't know you were a rat by now, this would clinch it. Who'd you have lunch with today?"

"Lunch? Oh—some character. A barfly I met last night. Name's Hartog. What's that got to do with—"

"Lie to the end, won't you? Well, it'll amaze you to know that I ducked into the bar at Roby's for a standup lunch today at one-thirty and saw you with my own eyes."

"You better get those eyes retreaded," snarled Killilea. "Why didn't you take the trouble to walk over and make sure?"

"If I ever got close enough to Jules Croy to talk to him, I'd tear his head off. And from now on the same goes for you. And if I hear one syllable from you on this phone again, I'll slam this thing down so hard I'll shunt it clear down to your end."

This time Killilea was ready, and had the receiver away from his ear when the crash came.

"It seems," he told Prue tiredly, "that I was seen having lunch with an arch-villain, who has tainted me. I didn't have lunch with anyone but the man you saw. Hartog."

"I don't like him," Prue said, for the second time that day. "Who was the villain?"

"Name's Croy, Jules Croy," said Killilea. Prue shook her head vaguely. "I've heard of him. One of those business octopi, finger in this, fifty thousand shares in that. Always buying up educators and research people with bequests. Egmont says he's trying to make a sort of glorified Parent-Teacher's Association out of what's left of the Ethical Science Board. Egg's always been real passionate about the Board, and it was like losing an arm to him when it folded. I guess he needed something to be real mad at, and the idea of me spying for this Croy supplied it."

"What about this man you had lunch with, this Hartog?"

"Oh, he's harmless. Interesting sometimes, the way one of those medical museums that feature replicas of skin diseases in life-size wax models is interesting. Did he give you a bad time?"

"Who—that little man?"

"I gather he made a series of passes. . . ."

"Oh," she said. "That. That never bothers me, Killy. You know that."

He knew it. When anyone irritated or bored her, she could leave the room without stirring from her chair. Her fogbound mood was absolutely impervious. "Oh," he said. "I thought . . . but you say he annoyed you."

"I didn't. I said I didn't like him. He . . . was the one who introduced me to Landey. And Koala—Dr. Pretorio—he knew him too. Koala and I once went to a party where he was. Compared to them, Hartog is such a little snipe."

"Knew Pretorio . . . hmm. Prue, did he know Karl Monck too?"

"I don't know. I don't think so. Killy, what is it?"

"Let me think . . . let me think." Suddenly he brought his hand down on the table, hard. "Prue! Hartog is the one who found you for me. He introduced himself to me at a bar down the street . . . let me see if I can remember exactly how . . . he questioned me in that funny way of his, I remember. He made sure of my name—yes, and—"

He looked down at his right palm. "What is it?" asked Prue, terror in her voice at the expression on his face.

"When we shook hands," he said evenly, "he scratched me. Look. With a ring he wore. A big cheap ring, the stone was missing, but the mounting had an edge."

Anger and terror mingled and mounted in the look they exchanged.

"I was right," she whispered. "You see . . . if I'd come home last night—oh, Killy!"

He looked at the hand. He felt as if he had been kicked in the stomach.

"Is there a—an antidote?"

He shook his head. "It's not the sort of thing that has an antidote. I mean, an acid poison can be counteracted by a base chemical of equal strength and opposite action. But things like this—hormones, for example. Progesterone and testosterone have opposite end effects, but a very similar way of bringing them about. I've never made any of this stuff, you know. I can't tell exactly how it acts or how long it lasts unless I do. It would surely have an active period, and then get absorbed and excreted like any hormone. How long that would be, I don't really know. I've got to develop a test for it. Another test for it," he said, giving her a painful grin.

"Well, at least we know. Now—this nasty little Hartog. Do you suppose Egmont was right? Could he really be this Jules Croy?"

"I guess he could. I'm trying to recall what happened to-day, at lunch. He came in—yes, that's right, he saw me and stopped dead, and I never saw a more astonished man."

"He sent you to me last night, didn't he? He must have known you were looking for me. He cut you with his ring, and he told you where I was, and he must have been sure that—no wonder he was astonished! You shouldn't have been alive today! Well—what did he say?"

"An involved sort of philosophic conversation. As usual with him, it was about sex." He thought back. "What it amounted to, was an attempt to pump me for information about you, and when that drew a blank, an effort to find some other woman for me, and then some delving into why I wasn't at all interested. It all fits," he said, almost awed. "The warped, wealthy little misfit, trying to buy his way into the high levels of science, trying to get control of the Ethical Science Board, removing the men who would have no use for his kind. He'll run it, Prue—it'll still attract every real scientist who has more humanity than a milling machine—and the men he can't control he'll eliminate. He has my factor as a weapon, and if that ever doesn't work, he can certainly think of other ways."

"The factor—how did he get it?"

"That's the one thing I can't figure," Killilea said grimly.

"We'll ask him." He looked at his watch. "Come on. We have things to do. I need a laboratory."

The first part was easy.

It was two nights later. Prue sat alone pale and unhappy-looking, at a table at Roby's. A cigarette burned to a long ash in the ashtray. An untouched drink stood warming in front of her. And—

"Well, hello," said Hartog.

"Oh," she said. She gave him a fleeting smile. He sat down quickly, opportunistically. "Expecting anyone?"

"No," she said.

"Oh," he said, in his ferocious, timid way. "Dined yet?"

"Not yet," she said. She took out a cigarette and waited. He fumbled in his pockets, and she glanced at the silver lighter lying next to her cigarettes. He mumbled an apology, picked it up, used it. When he put it down he looked puzzledly at his thumb. "I'm glad you came," she said.

He was surprised and showed it. "I guess I'm glad too," he said. He circled his thumb with his other hand and might have pressed it, but she reached out impulsively and took one of his hands in hers. "You haven't ever really talked to me," she said softly. "You've never given me a chance to really know you."

He talked, then, and when the conversation edged over to his preoccupation, it found her unperturbed. They dined. Afterward he said he felt strange. She said she had a little apartment nearby. Perhaps he'd be more comfortable there. . . .

She took him home.

She took his hat and coat and made him a drink and softly asked permission to change, and slipped into the bedroom. Hartog sat and sipped his drink and when he heard a sound behind him he said, "Come sit by me."

"All right," said Killilea.

Hartog came up off the couch as if it had contained a spark coil. Killilea circled the couch and pushed his chest. Hartog sat down again.

"Wh-what is this? The old badger game?"

"A much better game than that, Croy," said Killilea.

"Croy?"

"Your not going to deny it," said Killilea flatly. "Can you use a jeweler's loupe?"

"Use a what? What are you talking about? What is all this?"

"Here," said Killilea. Hartog took the loupe hesitatingly.

"I want to show you something." Killilea scooped the silver lighter off the end table and sat down close to Hartog. He raised the snuffer-lid of the lighter and held it close to Hartog's face. "Look through the loupe. Look right there, at the spark wheel."

Hartog stared at him then screwed the loupe into his eye. Killilea took out a mechanical pencil and pointed with it. "Watch right there." With the tip of his finger on the side— not the rim—of the spark wheel, he turned it. "See it, Croy?"

"No. Yes I do. A little hair."

"Not a hair. A needle."

"It worked fine, Killy," said Prue from the bedroom doorway. She had not changed. "He barely felt it."

"A little more refined than cutting someone with a finger ring," said Killilea.

"What have you done to me? Let me out of here!"

"What did you do to him?" Prue asked coldly of Hartog, pointing at Killilea.

"Is this some sort of a joke? I told you I was sorry about cutting you. What sort of childish—"

"Shut up, Croy," said Killilea tiredly. "I know who you are and what you're up to."

"I don't know what you mean. Why are you calling me Croy? What do you want from me?"

"Not a thing. Not a thing in the world." Killilea crossed to the door and locked it. "Just sit there and take it easy."

"You know your biochemistry," said Prue. "You're going to have heart failure, poor man."

Hartog looked at his thumb. "You mean you . . . that this is going to—why, you idiot, that won't work unless I—" he stopped.

Killilea grinned coldly. "Unless you what?" When Hartog didn't answer, Killilea said, "Hospitality has its limits, after all. Much as we enjoy company . . ." The bantering dropped out of his voice. "You have the wrong idea. You're going to die, Croy. In a half hour or so. I didn't have the time or the apparatus to make up the factor you used on me. You've got a dose of nice, simple, undetectable hormone poison."

"No!" gasped Hartog. "You *can't!* You mustn't! You've got this all wrong, Killilea. I swear it! I'm not what you think I am. . . ."

"Yes you are," said Killilea blackly. "I think you're a megalomaniac name of Jules Croy. I think you got on to my research in hormone-complex analogies. I think you used it to make some of the deadliest, most hellish extract that ever appeared on this earth. I'm sure that besides myself no one but you knows about it, and inside the hour no one but I will have it. It will be safe with me."

"What are you going to do with it?" Hartog asked faintly.

"Forget it. Pretend it never existed. . . . I see you're not denying anything any more."

"I'm Croy," said the man, with his eyes closed. "You're doing the right thing with the factor. But you're wrong about me. Believe me, you are. And you're wrong about no one else knowing."

Killilea caught his breath. "Who else knows?" He demanded.

"I can't tell you that."

"He's lying," said Killilea. "Croy, we have thirty minutes or so to kill, and there's nothing that can save you now. Why go out full of lies? Why not tell the truth?"

"There's nothing you could do if I did . . . it's too late now. I'm the only one who could help." He looked up at them piteously. "Am I going to die? Am I really going to die?"

Killilea nodded.

"It's a hard idea to get used to," Croy said, as if to himself.

"Tough," said Killilea. He wiped his forehead. "If you think we're enjoying this, we're not."

"I know that," said Croy surprisingly.

"You're taking this better than I thought you would."

"Am I? I hate the idea of dying—no, I don't. It's the idea of being dead I hate."

"Still the barroom philosopher," Killilea sneered.

"Don't," said Prue. "We don't have to hurt him, Killy. We just want him dead."

"Thanks," said Croy. He looked at Killilea. "I'm going to tell you everything. I don't expect you to believe it. You will, though. That won't help me, of course; I'll be dead several weeks by that time. But as you say, I have a few minutes to kill . . ."

He lay back. Sweat glistened on his upper lip. "You give me too much credit. I'm no scientist. I wouldn't know a ketosteroid from castor oil. I'm just a little man with a big bank account. I s'pose everyone has his poses. My analyst once told me I had a Haroun-al-Raschid pattern. Dressing up in cheap clothes and pretending to be something less than I was . . . giving sums of money secretly to this one and that one, not to help, just to *affect* people. Intrigues, secrets . . .

the breath of life to me. Breath of life . . . I feel awful. Is that symptomatic or psychosomatic?"

"Symptomatic," said Killilea. "Go on. If you want to."

"It was Pretorio who got on to what you were doing. One of the few real all-around scientists in this century. Immense ability to extrapolate. He saw the directions your researches were taking you, and he got alarmed when you quit reporting progress but kept on working."

"But how did he *know?*"

"Through me. I own Zwing & Rockwood."

Killilea clapped a hand to his head. "I *never* thought of that!"

"What, Killy? Who's Zwing and Rockwood?"

"Glassblowers! Work like mine calls for very special custom apparatus. And step by step, as I ordered apparatus—"

"That's it," nodded Croy. "For Pretorio it wasn't too tough. He was working right along with you the whole time. Sometimes he was ahead. Sometimes he would call and tell me exactly what piece of glass you'd order next."

"I *thought* I was getting fantastically good service."

"You were."

"What on earth was Pretorio after? Why didn't he come to me? How did you happen to be working with him?"

"What was he after? What he told me was that he was afraid you didn't know the possibilities of what you were doing. He was so afraid of it that he didn't want to tip you off by asking you. After all, he was the great extrapolator, you know. As for me, I was flattered. He had me completely spellbound. You just don't know what a tremendous man he was, what an—an aura he had."

"I do," said Prue.

"I did absolutely everything he told me to do. Some of it I couldn't understand, but I trusted him completely."

"And then he died."

"I went sort of crazy after that, I guess. Didn't know what to do with myself. It was pretty bad. Then one day I got a call from a man with a husky voice. He said Pretorio had left him instructions. I didn't believe him at first, but when he started giving me details that no one but Pretorio could have told him, I had to believe."

"Who was he?"

"He never told me. I never met him. He said it had to be that way because he hadn't Pretorio's great reputation. But Pretorio's work had to go on. Well, I followed orders. You know about Landey, and then Monck. I was blind, stupid, I guess. You'll have to take my word for it that I injected both of them and introduced them to her—" he indicated Prue with his chin—"without knowing why they were dying. I thought it was heart failure, just like everyone else. I didn't even know she was with them when they died."

"What about Pretorio? You infected him, didn't you?"

"No, damn it, I didn't!" shouted Croy, his voice angry for the first time since he had started his narrative. "That must have been an accident—the one crazy accident that fell in line with the things I arranged. Or maybe he injected himself by accident. It doesn't take much, you know."

"I know," said Killilea grimly.

"Well, the day came when I got orders to do the same for you. I didn't know until then who she was. When I found that out I got some thinking done. It was like coming up out of a dream. I'd never doubted this man's word any more than I had Pretorio's, but now I did. I saw then what these deaths meant; I connected them with the Ethical Science Board that I was supposed to take over and run for this man; I saw suddenly how you four—Pretorio, Landey, Monck and yourself would have stood in his way. I called him back and refused to go on with him.

"He told me then what he was after. He told me what the factor was, what it could do, how the world had to be protected from it. He told me that you developed it, that unless you were stopped it would slip out of your hands and plunge the world into ruin. And about the Board, he said the world wasn't ready for a group that would efficiently cross-fertilize scientific specialties. We haven't caught up, as a culture, with the science we already have.

"I agreed with him and promised to go on."

"Why—the man is crazy! And so are you, for swallowing that drivel!"

"Who swallowed it? I knew then he was crazy, that he was responsible for the death of one of the finest men since Leonardo, that he'd made a murderer out of me and put you two through hell . . . so I made up my mind to play along with him until I could find out who he was. I was ready to kill him, but how do you kill a man unless you can find him, and how do you find him when you don't know his name or what he looks like?" He spread his hands, dropped them. "And that's all. I know it looks bad for me, and I guess I've earned what I'm getting. But—like I said . . . no one but me can find him, and by the time you get proof of that I'll be dead. He's going to kill you, you know. He's got to.

He can't afford to have anyone else know about the factor."

Killilea strode across to the sofa and lifted a heavy fist. "Killy!" cried Prue.

With difficulty Killilea lowered the fist. "You're a liar," he said thickly. "If that ingenious story is true, why did you cut my hand with the ring?"

"I told you. I had to play it his way. But I didn't inject the factor! It was something else—something that may have saved your life. Progesterone."

"Why on earth progesterone?"

"Orders were to tell you where *she* was, see to it you went to her. You were looking for her; you wanted her back. It was a wonderful setup for his plan. I didn't know too much about hormones, but I did what I could. I had the stuff compounded; progesterone and a large charge of SF—hyaluronidase, I think it was—to make it spread."

"What on earth is that?" asked Prue.

"An enzyme. SF means 'spreading factor,'" said Killilea. "Lectures later, Prue. Go on, Croy."

"You had enough progesterone in you to bank your fire for a week," said Croy. "By that time I hoped to have the whole thing cracked."

"You sure were upset when you found me alive the next day."

"I was upset when I found you were there. I wanted to get you out of my sight. I didn't know when my—my would-be boss might see you."

"Then why all the talk about finding me another chick?"

"I wanted to see if the hormone was working. I wanted to find out where you stood with *her*. But when she came in, there was nothing I could do. It was all right, anyway. As long as you were together, he could assume only that you were taking your time in making peace."

"An answer for everything," said Killilea. "How much of this do you believe, Prue?"

"I don't know," she said, troubled. To Croy she said, "Why didn't you tell us this before? Why didn't you tell me tonight at dinner? Or even after you found Killy here?"

"Do you know of a scientist worth his salt that would even speak to me?" Croy said wistfully. "The first chance I ever had to do something really fine for science—I wasn't going to jeopardize that by getting slapped down when you found out who I was. Don't you see that's why I was so pleased to be able to work with Pretorio?"

"I remember what Egmont said about him," mused Killilea.

"Egmont," said Croy. "The crystallographer? Yes; a good case in point. He can't stand the sight of me. When he found out I was behind the scenes in the Board membership I thought he would explode."

"He did explode," said Killilea. "Prue, we've got quite a story to tell the Egg."

"There'll be time for that later. Killy, suppose he's right? Suppose there really is someone else who knows about your factor—someone as dangerous as Croy says?"

"We'll hear from him," said Killilea.

"He won't be as clumsy as I was," said Croy. "I tell you you'll be dead before you know who killed you."

"I guess I'll have to chance it," said Killilea. "You said if you lived you could find him for us. At least you can tell us how, so we can try."

"There would be only one way—to trace him when he calls me. He won't call me after I'm dead."

Killilea watched Croy narrowly. "If you had a chance to catch him now, would you do it?"

"Would I! If I only could!"

"We've killed you," Prue pointed out.

"You did what you could; you were right as far as you knew. And I suppose I have to pay for what I've done . . . I'm not angry at you two."

"All right then. Either you're the cleverest liar or one of the bravest men I've ever met," said Killilea. "Now I'm going to remind you of something. You said that when he ordered you to inject me with the factor, you balked. *You called him back.* Give us that phone number and you've proved your point."

"The phone number," Croy breathed. "It hadn't occurred to me because he always said it was useless to call except in the afternoon; he wouldn't be there at any other time."

"Ever try it?"

"No."

Killilea pointed to the phone. "Try it."

"What shall I say?"

There was a heavy silence. "Get him here."

"He wouldn't come here."

"He would if his whole plan depended on it," said Killilea. "Come on, Croy. You're the boy for intrigue."

Croy put his head in his hands.

"I knew he'd balk," snarled Killilea.

"Shut up," said Croy, startlingly. "Let me think."

He crouched there. He covered his eyes, then suddenly raised his head. "Give me the phone."

"Better tell us first what you're going to say."

"Oh, Killy," said Prue, "stop acting like a big bad private detective! Let him do it his way!"

"No," said Killilea. "He's dying, Prue. And if he isn't half-cracked just now, we know he has been. How do we know he isn't going to pull us in the hole after him?"

"Phone him," said Prue evenly.

Croy looked from one to the other, then took the phone from the end table. From his wallet he took a piece of paper and dialed. "You better be right," Killilea whispered to Prue. He went to Croy and took the paper out of his hand and put it in his own pocket. Through the silent room the sound of the ringing signal rasped at them. At the sixth unanswered ring Killilea said, "Even if he's there now—oh, Prue, it might be just a trick. . . ."

Croy covered the transmitter. "I haven't time for tricks," he said. And just then the receiver clicked, and a hoarse voice said, "Well?"

Prue gripped Killilea's biceps so hard that he all but grunted. Croy, pale but steady, said, "I'm in trouble."

"It better be bad trouble," said the voice. "I told you not to call me this late."

"It's bad, right enough," said Croy. The reversion to an English accent under strain was quite noticeable. "She took me to her apartment. Killilea was here."

"Alive?"

"I should say so. Alive and very much aware of what's happening. I hit him with the poker."

"Go hit him again."

"I can't—I can't do that. Besides, he told her everything. She knows, now, too."

"Where is she?"

"Tied up. What shall I do?"

A long pause. No one breathed. "I'll come over. Where is it?"

Croy gave the address and apartment number. "And hurry. I don't know how long he'll stay under. Take you long?"

"Fifteen minutes." *Click.* Croy looked up at them. "Have I got fifteen minutes?" he asked. His face was wet.

Killilea looked at his watch. "How do you feel?"

"Not good."

Killilea went into the bedroom and came out a moment later with a hypodermic in his hand. "Lie down," he said.

"Relax. Relax," he said again, touching the side of Croy's neck, "completely. Better." He slid the left sleeve up, squirted a drop of fluid upward from the needle, and buried the gleaming point in the large vein inside the elbow. "Just take it easy until he gets here. You'll last."

"What is it?"

"Adrenalin."

Croy closed his eyes. His lips were slightly cyanotic and his breathing was shallow.

"Are you sure he'll last?" asked Prue.

"Sure." Killilea smiled tightly. "Believe him?"

"Mostly, I think."

"Me too. Mostly. We could be making an awful mistake, Prue."

"Mmm. Either way."

He took a turn up and down the room. "Morals and ethics," he said. "You never really know, do you?"

"You do the best you can," she said. "Killy, you do very well indeed."

"Do I?"

"You react ethically much oftener than morally. You react ethically as much as other people do morally."

"What are you thinking about?"

"Killy, you never said a word to me about what I did. With those men, Karl and the Koala. . . ."

"What word should I say?"

She looked at her hands. "You've read books. Insane jealousies and bitterness and distrust. . . ."

"Oh," he said. He thought hard for a moment. "The things you did were . . . just little, unimportant, corroborative details. The big thing was that you had gone. I didn't like your going. But I didn't feel that a part of me was doing those things; which is the feeling jealous people have. You didn't stray when you were with me. You won't when you come back."

"No," she said almost inaudibly. "I won't. But, Killy, that's what I mean when I say you don't react morally. Morals, per se, would have killed what we have together. Ethics—and here it's just another name for our respect for one another—have saved it. Another argument for the higher survival value of ethics."

They sat quietly then, together in the easy chair that was built for one, and were quiet, until Killilea looked at his watch, extricated himself from the chair, and went to Croy.

"It's almost time, Croy," he said levelly. "Go into your act. You feel up to it?"

Croy swung his feet down and shook his head violently. "My face is made of rubber and my heart thinks I'm running the three hundred meter," he said. "I'll make it, though."

"Come on, Prue."

They went into the bedroom, turned out the light, and closed the door until just a finger's breadth of golden light showed from the living room lamp.

They waited.

The doorbell rang. Croy started for the door. "That's downstairs," Killilea murmured. "Push the button in the kitchenette. And don't forget the door here is locked when you try to open it. Speak fairly loud so he will too. I'll take your cues. And Croy, God help you if—"

Prue's hand slid up and covered his mouth. "Good luck, Mr. Croy," she said.

The buzzer hissed like a snake. Croy drew a deep breath, crossed the room, unlocked the door and opened it. "Where are they?" said a hoarse voice.

"In there," said Croy, "but wait . . . what are you going to do?"

"What do you expect?" said the newcomer. Killilea could see him now—short, heavy, almost chinless; wide forehead, low hairline.

"You're going to kill them," said Croy.

"Do you have a better idea?"

"Have you thought about the details—what happens when the bodies are found, what will the police do?"

The stranger opened his overcoat and from what must have been a special pocket drew out a leather-covered wooden case. He set it on the table, opened it, and took out a hypodermic. He grinned briefly. "Heart failure. So common nowadays."

"Two cases at once?"

"Hmm. You have something there. Well . . . I can take one of them away in my car."

"I was wondering," Croy said tightly, "if you'd expect me to do it."

The man regarded him without expression. "It's a possibility."

"It would mean I'd have to leave here alive. You wouldn't want that, would you?"

The man laughed. "Oh, I see! My dear fellow, you needn't

fear for yourself. Aside from considerations of friendship—even admiration—I couldn't possibly complete my plans for the Board without you."

Killilea, his eye fixed to the crack of the door, felt an urgent tugging at his shoulder. Killilea backed away and let her work her way silently around him so that she could see as well.

The man started toward the bedroom. Croy said evenly, "Where have I seen you before?"

The man stopped without turning. The needle glinted in his hand. "I have no idea. I doubt that you ever have."

"I have, though. I have—someplace. . . ."

Prue gasped suddenly. Killilea took her shoulders and with one easy motion flung her through the air. She landed on the middle of the bed. The gasp alerted their visitor who dove for the door. Killilea stepped aside and let it crash open. Light from the living room flooded the man's broad back as he stopped, blinking, in the darkness, peering from one side to the other. Killilea stood up on tiptoe and with all his strength brought the edge of his right hand down on the nape of the man's neck. He went down flat with no sound but his falling, and lay still.

Killilea was gasping as if he had run up steps. He bent and lifted the man's shoulder. It fell back loosely. "Out, all right," said Killilea. "Prue, what got into you? You almost gave us away by making that silly—Prue! What—"

She sat on the edge of the bed, her hands over her face, shuddering. He put his arms around her. "It's Koala," she said. "Oh, Killy, it's Koala. . . ."

Croy was standing white-faced in the doorway. "What's she say? What's koala mean?"

"It means a great deal. Turn him over and look at him, Croy. Maybe you'll remember where you saw him."

Croy bent down and rolled the heavy body over. "He's dead!"

Killilea left the bed and ran to Croy, knelt down. "Yeah," he said. "Yeah." He picked up a broken tube of glass, looked at it, laid it down on the carpet. Then he began running his fingers lightly over the front of the man's coat.

"Careful," said Croy.

"Oh, but yes. Here it is." Slowly and cautiously he unbuttoned jacket, vest and shirt. The undershirt showed a small bloodspot, just a drop. From its center extended the needle. Using his handkerchief folded twice, Killilea grasped it and pulled it out. It had penetrated only a fraction of an inch. "Far enough," said Killilea and Croy gave an understanding grunt.

"Heart trouble," said Killilea.

Croy said, "You're still going to have . . . two bodies . . . to explain. And you don't even know who this one is."

"Yes I do," said Killilea. "You do too, if you'll only look at him." He bent close. "Brown-tinted contact lenses," he said. "I think his eyes are blue. Right, Prue?"

She gave a long, shuddering sigh. "Yes," she whispered. "And he had a beard to hide that little chin."

"Beard," said Croy, and then dropped to his knees. *"Dr. Pretorio!"*

"It had to be. Now I feel like the boys at that dinner table where Columbus demonstrated how to stand an egg on end."

"But he's . . . he was dead!"

"When we get his coffin dug up—if we bother—we'll find out who really was buried at Pretorio's funeral," said Killilea. "If anyone."

"Why?" moaned Croy.

Killilea stood up and dusted off his hands. "Thought a lot of him, didn't you, Croy? Why did he do it? I guess we'll never know in detail. But I'd say his mind snapped. He got afraid of the Board, really his own creation, when he discovered my factor, and wanted it for himself. The Board needed wrecking, and he threw his own supposed death on the wreckage, along with his great reputation. A mind like that, working against society instead of for it, would be happier operating underground. I wonder what he would have done with the factor?"

"He told me last week that the reorganized Board could run the world," said Croy in a small voice. "I thought he was flattering me. I thought it was a figure of speech. Oh, God. Pretorio." Tears ran down his face.

"You'll have to give me a hand," said Killilea. "We'll get him down to his car and leave him in it. And that will be that."

"All right . . . do I have time?" asked Croy.

Killilea came to him. "Let's see your tongue. Mmmm-hm!" He lifted Croy's damp wrist and looked thoughtful. "In your condition I'd give you about forty more years."

Croy simply looked at him blankly. Killilea slapped him on the shoulder. "Maybe it's morals, and maybe it's ethics," he said kindly, "but neither Prue nor I could sit and talk while we watched a man die. You got an injection of dilute caffeine citrate to sweat you up, and some adrenalin to make you tingle."

Croy's jaw opened and closed ludicrously. At last he said, "But I'm supposed to . . . I have to pay for . . . ."

Killilea laughed. "Listen, philosopher. If you really feel nice and guilty and want to get punished—live with it, don't die for it just so you can escape all those sleepless nights."

Then Croy began to laugh . . . .

Together they got the heavy body downstairs while Prue scouted ahead. They saw no one, though they had a drunken-friend story ready. They arranged the corpse carefully behind the wheel and left it.

Back in the foyer of the apartment house, Killilea asked, "Which way do you go?"

"Bilville."

"You can't go all the way out there this late!" Prue cried. "Go back up stairs. You can make yourself quite comfortable there. There's orange juice in the refrigerator, and the clean towels are—"

"But won't you—"

"No," said Killilea flatly, "she won't. I'm taking my wife home."

Howard Browne bought this one, because, he said, he liked it. He must have found it a refuge from what he was doing at the time, for it is a strange and filmy kind of effort, whereas Howard, as "John Evans" was writing the (I think) third of a series of the hardest-heeling of all hardheel detective novels, all of which had the word "halo" in the title, and all of which featured a rocky little scut of a detective called Paul Pine. Howard has for some years now been basking in the never-setting sun (they got lamps) of Hollywood, and I'd love to see him again. He was a fine editor and a fine guy, and just to disprove that crack about editors being writers who can't make it, he's a writer who can and does.

Why doesn't someone reprint the 'Halo' books? They're great!

Make Room for Me

"WE SHALL never see him again. . . . there will be no more arguments, no more pleasant thinking with Eudiche," mourned Torth to the other Titan.

"Come now. Don't be so pessimistic," said Larit, stroking the machine. "The idea of dissociation has horrified you, that's all. There is every chance that his components will fuse."

"So involved, so very involved," Torth fretted. "Is there really no way to send the complete psyche?"

"Apparently not. The crystals are of a limited capacity, you know. If we grow them larger, they cannot retain a psychic particle. If we sent all three encased particles together, their interaction would break down the crystals chemically. They must be sent separately."

"But—horrible! How can one third of a psyche live alone?"

"Biologically, you know perfectly well. Psychologically, you need only look about you. You will find a single psyche only in each of our gracious hosts—"

"—gracious indeed," muttered Torth, "and gracious they will remain, or die."

"—and each of the natives on the planet to which we sent Eudiche has but one psyche."

"How then can he occupy three of them?"

"Torth, you insist on asking questions requiring a higher technological comprehension than yours to understand," replied the other in annoyance. "There are closer ties than physical proximity. Eudiche will avail himself of them. Let that suffice." More kindly, he added, "Eudiche will be all right. Wait; just wait."*

*   *   *

The statue of Ben Franklin, by the very weight of its greyness, sobered the green sparkle of the campus. At the foot of the benevolent image the trio stood—Vaughn, tiny, with long braids of flaxen hair; Dran, slender and aquiline, and—apart from the others, as usual—Manuel, with heavy shoulders and deep horizontal creases over his thick brows.

Dran smiled at some chattering coeds who passed, then slanted his narrow face toward the semi-circle of stone buildings. "After three years," he said, "I've gotten over being delighted by my own uniqueness—the three miserable years it took me to convince myself that distinction and difference are not synonymous. And now that I'm *of* this place—no longer on the outside looking in, or on the inside looking on, I—"

"Who's so exceptional?" growled Manuel, moving closer. "Aside from the runt here, who never will get the knack of being a human being."

"Are you a specimen of humanity?" asked the girl stormily. "Manuel, I don't expect compliments from you, but I wish you'd try courtesy. Now listen. I have something to tell you. I—"

"Wait a minute," said Dran, "I have something more important, whatever you have on your mind. I've got the answer—for me, anyway—to this whole question of being the same as everyone else and being different at the same time. I—"

"You said it all last night," said Vaughn wearily. "Only you were so full of sherry that you didn't know what you were saying. I quote: 'Vaughn, not only your charming person but your poetry would be a lot more popular if you

---

* The author apologizes for this poor translation of the Titan personal pronoun, which, in the original, is singular and plural, masculine and feminine, and has no counterpart in our tongue.

wouldn't hide behind this closed door of non-aggression and restraint.' Well, I've been thinking about that, and I—"

"Manuel," Dran interrupted, "you've got muscles. Throttle her, will you? Just a little. Just until I can put a predicate on this subject."

"I'd love to get started on that job," grinned Manuel, licking his lips. "Imagine how those wall eyes would pop."

"Keep your hands off me, animal," Vaughn hissed. "Dran, I'm trying to—"

"I will not be stopped," said Dran. With a gesture completely characteristic, he knocked back a strand of his red-gold hair, scattering ashes from his cigarette through it. "Be quiet and listen. You two have held still for a lot of my mouthings and gnashings of teeth about my being a white monkey—the one all the brown monkeys will tear to pieces just because he's different. Well, I have the solution."

"Get to the point," Manuel grunted. "It could be that I got a speech to make, too."

"Not until I've told you—" Vaughn began.

"Shut up, both of you," said Dran. "Especially you, Vaughn. All right. What are we here for?"

"To get a degree."

"We are not. At least, I'm not," said Dran. "The more I think of it, the less I think school teaches you anything. Oh, sure, there are some encyclopaedics that you sponge up, but that's secondary. A school's real function is to teach you how to learn. Period."

"All right—then what about the degree?"

"That's just to convince other people that you have learned how to learn. Or to convince yourself, if you're not sure. What I'm driving at, is that *I'm* sure. I know all I need to know about how to learn. I'm leaving."

There was a stunned silence. Vaughn looked slowly from one to the other. Dran's eyebrows went up. "I didn't expect such a dramatic effect. Vaughn . . . ? Say something!"

"Y-you've been reading my script!" she murmured. Her eyes were huge.

"What do you mean?"

"Why—I've been thinking . . . For more than a year I've known what I wanted to do. And this—" she waved a hand at the grey buildings— "this hasn't been it. This . . . interferes. And I wanted to tell you about that, and that you mustn't think it means that I've finished learning. I want to learn a world of things—but not here."

Manuel released a short bark of laughter. "You mean you made a great big decision—all by yourself?"

"I'll make a decision about you one of these days, now that I've learned the technique," she spat. "Dran . . . what are you going to do? Where are you going?"

"I have something lined up. Advertising—direct mail. It isn't too tough. I'll stay with that for a couple of years. See how the other half lives. The half with money, that is. When I'm ready, I'll drop it and write a novel. It'll be highly successful."

"Real cocky," said Manuel.

"Well, damn it, it will be. With me. *I'll* like it. So far as I'm concerned it will be successful. And what about you, Vaughn?"

"I have a little money. Not much. But I'll manage. I'll write poems." She smiled. "They'll be successful, too."

"Good thing you guys don't have to depend on what anyone else thinks," Manuel grunted. "Me, I do it the way the man wants it done or else."

"But you please yourself doing it," Dran said.

"Huh? I—never thought of it like that. I guess you're right. Well." He looked from Vaughn to Dran and back. They suddenly spoke, almost in unison. "Manuel! What are you going to—" and—"Manuel! What will you do now?"

"Me? I'll make out. You two don't think I *need* you?"

Vaughn's eyes grew bright. Dran put an understanding hand on her shoulder. He said, "Who writes this plot? What a switch! Manuel, of all people, clinging to these walls with the rest of the ivy, while Vaughn and I try our wings."

"Sometimes you characters give me a pain in the back of my lap," said Manuel abruptly. "I hang around with you and listen to simple-minded gobbledegook in yard-long language, if it's you talking, Dran, and pink-and-purple sissification from the brat here. Why I do it I'll never know. And it goes that way up to the last gasp. So you're going to leave. Dran has to make a speech, real logical. Vaughn has to blow out a sigh and get misty-eyed." He spat.

"How would you handle it?" Dran asked, amused. Vaughn stared at Manuel whitely.

"Me? You really want to know?"

"This I want to hear," said Vaughn between her teeth.

"I'd wait a while—a long while—until neither of you was talking. Then I'd say, 'I joined the Marines yesterday.' And you'd both look at me a little sad. There's supposed to be something wrong with coming right out and saying something. Let's see. Suppose I do it the way Vaughn would want me to." He tugged at an imaginary braid and thrust out his lower lip in a lampoon of Vaughn's full mouth. He sighed gustily. "I have felt . . ." He paused to flutter his eyelashes. "I have felt the call to arms," he said in a histrionic whisper. He gazed off into the middle distance. "I have heard the sound of trumpets. The drums stir in my blood." He pounded his temples with his fists. "I can't stand it—I can't! Glory beckons. I will away to foreign strands."

Vaughn turned on her heel, though she made no effort to walk away. Dran roared with laughter.

"And suppose I'm you," said Manuel, his face taut with a suppressed grin. He leaned easily against the base of the statue and crossed his legs. He flung his head back. "Zeno of Miletus," he intoned, "in reflecting on the cromislon of the fortiseetus, was wont to refer to a razor as 'a check for a short beard.' While shaving this morning I correlated 'lather' with 'leather' and, seeing some of it on my neck, I recalled the old French proverb, *'Jeanne D'Arc'*, which means: The light is out in the bathroom. The integration was complete. If the light was out I could no longer shave. Therefore I can not go on like this. Also there was this matter of the neck. I shall join the Marines. Q. E. D., which means thus spake Zarathusiasm."

Dran chuckled. Vaughn made a furious effort, failed, and burst out laughing. When it subsided, Manuel said soberly, "I did."

"You did what?"

"I joined the Marines yesterday."

Dran paled. Manuel looked at him in open astonishment. He had never seen Dran without an instant response before. And Vaughn clutched at his arms. "You didn't! You couldn't! Manuel . . . Manuel . . . the uniform . . . the pain . . . you'll be *killed!*"

"Yup. But slowly. In agony. And as I lie there in the growing dark, a sweet thought will sustain me. I'll never again see another line of your lousy poetry. For Christ's sake!" he bellowed suddenly, "Get off that tragic kick, stupid! I'll be all right."

"What did you go and do a thing like that for?" Dran asked slowly.

"What are you and the reptile leaving for?" Manuel returned. "The same thing. This place has taught me all it can—for me. I'm going where I'll know who's my boss, and I'll know who takes orders from me. What I'll wear, where I'll live—someone else can decide that. Meantime I'll work in communications, which I'd be doing anyway, but someone else will buy the equipment and materials."

"You'll be caged. You'll never be free," said Vaughn.

"Free for what? To starve? Free to argue with salesmen and landlords? Nuts. I'll go and work with things I can measure, work with my hands, while you two are ex-prassing your tortured souls. What would you like to see me do instead? Take up writing sonnets that nobody'll ever read? Suppose I do that, and *you* go join the Marines."

Dran touched Vaughn's arm. "He's right, Vaughn. What he's doing would be wrong for you, or for me, but it's right for him."

"I don't . . . I don't know what to do," she mourned.

"I do," said Manuel. "Let's go eat."

*　*　*

"We are parasites," said the Titan, "which is the initial measure of our intelligence."

Torth said, "Our intelligence doesn't make it possible for us to survive on Titan."

"It's an impasse. The very act of settling the three components of our psyche into the brains of the natives gives us a home—and shortens the life of the native."

"Wouldn't that be true of the bipeds on the third planet?"

"To a degree," admitted the other. "But they are long-lived—and there are three billion of them."

"And how would we affect them?"

"Just as we affect the natives here."

Torth made the emanation which signified amusement. "That should make them very unhappy."

"You speak of a matter of no importance," said the other irritably. "And it is not true. They will be as incapable of expressing unhappiness as anything else." He applied himself again to the machine, with which he was tracking the three crystalline casings which carried Eudiche on his earthward journey.

*　*　*

After dinner they went to a concert. They sat in their favorite seats—the loges—and waited, each wrapped in his own thoughts. Dran stared at the dusty carved figures under the ceiling. Manuel sketched busily—a power-operated shock absorber, this time. Between them Vaughn sat, withdrawn and dreamy, turning night-thoughts into free verse.

They straightened as the conductor appeared and crossed the platform, amid applause which sounded like dead leaves under his feet. When he raised his baton, Vaughn glanced swiftly at the faces of the other two, and then they pressed forward in unison.

It was Bach—the *Passacaglia* and *Fugue in C Minor*. The music stepped and spiralled solemnly around them, enclosing them in a splendid privacy. They were separate from the rest of the audience, drawn to each other. Manuel and Dran moved slightly toward Vaughn, until their shoulders touched. Their eyes fixed unmoving on the orchestra.

At the last balanced, benevolent crescendo they rose together and left, ahead of the crowd. None of them cared to talk, strangely. They walked swiftly through the dark streets to a brightly lit little restaurant several blocks from the Academy.

In a high-walled booth, they smiled to each other as if acknowledging a rich secret. Then Vaughn's eyes dropped; she pulled at her fingers and sighed.

"No effusions from you, please," said Dran—possibly more coldly than he intended. "We all felt it, whatever it was. Don't mess it up."

Vaughn's gaze was up again, shocked. Manuel said, with an astonishing gentleness, with difficulty, "I was—somewhere else, but you were with me. And we all seemed to be— to be walking, or climbing . . ." He shook his massive head. "Nuts. I must be thirsty or something. What do you want, runt? Dran?"

Vaughn didn't answer. She was staring at Dran, her violet eyes dark with hurt.

"Speak up, chicken. I didn't mean to crush you. I just didn't feel like listening to an iambic extravagance. Something happened to all of us."

"Thanks f-for crediting me with so little sensitivity that you think I didn't feel it. That you think I'd spoil it!"

"Not too little sensitivity. Too much—*and* out of control. I'm sorry," Dran relented. "Let's order." He turned to Manuel, and froze in surprise at the look in the other's face. It was a look of struggling, as if unwelcome forces were waking within him, disturbing the rough, familiar patterns of his thinking.

Joe passed, flashy, noisy, wide open for hurt. The trio had

often discussed Joe. Superficially, he was pushing into their group because of Vaughn, who appeared to make him quite breathless. Dran had once said however, that it went deeper than that. Joe could not abide a liaison that he couldn't understand. Joe called, "Hi! As I live and bleed, it's the internal triangle. Nice to see you, Vaughn. When am I going to do it on purpose instead of by accident?"

"Is this drip necessary?" Manuel muttered.

"I'll see you soon, Joe," Vaughn said, smiling at him. "We have a class together tomorrow. I'll talk to you about it then." Her nod was a warm touch, and a dismissal. Joe appeared about to speak, thought better of it, waved and went away.

"That impossible idiot," growled Dran. "A more quintessential jerk I have yet to meet."

"Oh, Dran! He's not bad! Just undeveloped. Of course, he isn't one of *us*, but he's fun all the same. He reads good poetry, and he's quite a—"

Manuel brought his hand down with a crash. *"That's* what I was after. 'One of us.' What do you mean, 'one of us?' Who joins this union? I'm not 'one of us.' You two have more in common than you have with me."

Vaughn touched his hand. "Manuel," she said softly. "Oh, Manuel! Why, everyone links us together. I—I know I do. So much so that until now I didn't think it required questioning. It's something you accept as natural."

Dran's eyes brightened. "Wait, Vaughn. Let's not call it natural. Let's examine it. See what we get. I've been chewing on it since the business with the music tonight anyway."

Manuel shrugged. "Okay. What do the runt and I share after all? You and I can agree on politics, and we have one or two mechanical interests. But you, Vaughn—you . . ." He wet his lips. "Hell!" he exploded. "You're—useless!"

"I can ignore that," said Vaughn, very obviously ignoring nothing, "because you are only trying to hurt me."

"Hold on," said Dran easily. "I think this is worth an effort to avoid that kind of emotional smokescreen. You particularly, Manny. You sound resentful, and I don't know that you have anything to resent."

"She makes me mad, that's all. Look—there are a lot of useful things in the world—lock washers . . . cotter pins. But this—this dame! You couldn't use her for a paperweight. She's a worm trying to be a snake. You can't approach her logically. I can get to you that way, Dran, though I'll admit the going gets a little swampy sometimes."

"Perhaps this thing we have," said Vaughn softly, "is more than emotion, or intellect, or any of those things."

"Here we go again," snorted Manuel.

"A mystic entity or something?" Dran chuckled. "I doubt it. But there is something between us—all of us. It isn't limited to any two. We all belong. I'm not sure of what it's for, or even if I like it. But I'm not prepared to deny it. You aren't either, Manny."

"Manuel," said Vaughn urgently. She reached across and touched him, as if she wanted to press her eager words into him. "Manuel—haven't you ever felt it even a little? Didn't you, tonight? Didn't you? In your own terms. . . . Manuel, just this once, I'd like to know honestly, without any sneers."

Manuel glowered at her, hesitated, then said, "What if I have?" truculently. In a gentler tone, he added, "Oh, I have, all right. Once or twice. It—like I said, damn it, it makes me mad. I don't like getting pushed around by something I don't understand. It'll probably stop when I get away from here, and good riddance to it."

Vaughn touched her knuckles to her teeth. She whispered, "To me, it's something to treasure."

Dran grinned at her. "If you like it it's got to be fragile, hm? Vaughn, it isn't. And I think Manny's in for a surprise if he thinks distance is going to make any difference."

"I have hopes," Manuel said sullenly.

Dran spread his hands on the table and looked at them. "Vaughn stands in awe of this—this thing we have, and to Manuel it's like a dose of crabs. Excuse me, chicken. Far as I'm concerned, it's something that will bear watching. I can't analyze it now. If it gets weaker I will be able to analyze it even less. If it gets stronger it will show its nature no matter what I do. So I'm going to relax and enjoy it. I can say this much . . ." He paused, frowning, searching for words. "There is a lowest common denominator for us. We're all 'way off balance. And our imbalances are utterly different in kind, and negligibly different in degree."

Vaughn stared dully. Manuel said, "Huh?"

Dran said, more carefully, "Vaughn's all pastels and poetry. Manuel's all tools and technology. I'm—"

"All crap and complication," said Manuel.

"Manuel!"

Dran laughed. "He's probably right, Vaughn. Anyway, we're all lopsided to the same degree, which is a lot, and that's the only real similarity between us. If we three were one person, it'd be a somebody, that's for sure."

"It'd be an insect," Manuel scowled. "Six legs." He looked at Vaughn. "With your head. No one'd know the difference."

"You're ichor-noclastic," said Dran. Vaughn groaned. Manuel said, "That was one of those puns. The only part I got was the 'corn'. Where the hell's the waiter?"

* * *

"Why Eudiche?" Torth fretted. "Why couldn't they send someone else?"

"Eudiche is expendable," said the other parasite shortly.

"Why? His balance is so perfect . . ."

"Answer restricted. Go away. One-third of his psyche has found a host and is settling in. The observations are exceedingly difficult, because of the subtlety of Eudiche's operations. And you are most exasperating."

* * *

For the third time in a week, Vaughn was lunching with Joe—a remarkable thing, considering that in the two years since her departure from the University she had seen less and less of old acquaintances. But after all—Joe was easy to be with because she didn't have to pretend. She could be as moody as she chose. He would patiently listen to her long and misty reflections, and let her recite poetry without protest. The meetings did not hurt her, and Joe seemed to enjoy them so. . . .

But Joe had something to offer this time, rather than something to take. As the waitress took their dessert order and left, he gently placed a little plush box beside her coffee cup. "Won't you consider it at all?" he asked diffidently.

Her hand was on the box, reflexively, before she realized what it was. Then she looked at him. Thoughts, feelings, swirled about each other within her, like petals, paper, dust and moths in a small sudden whirlwind. Her eyes fixed on his shy, anxious face, and she realized that she had seldom looked directly at him . . . and that he was good to look at. She looked at the box and back at him, and then closed her violet eyes. Joe as a suitor, as a potential lover, was an utterly new idea to her. Joe as a bright-faced, carefully considerate *thing* was not Joe with hands, Joe with a body, Joe with habit patterns and a career and toothpaste and beneficiaries for life insurance. She felt flattered and bewildered and uncertain, and—warm.

And then something happened. It was as if an indefinable presence had raised its head and was listening. This alien attentiveness added a facet to the consideration of Joe. It made the acceptance or rejection of Joe a more significant thing than it had been. The warmth was still there, but it was gradually overlaid by a—a knowledge that created a special caution, a particular inviolability.

She smiled softly then, and her hand lifted away from the box.

"There's nothing final about an engagement," Joe said. "It would be up to you. Every minute. You could give me back the ring any time. I'd never ask you why. I'd understand, or try to."

"Joe." She put out her hand, almost touched him, then drew it back. "I . . . you're so *very* sweet, and this is a splendid compliment. But I can't do it. I—If I succeeded in persuading myself into it, I'd only regret it, and punish you."

"Umm," mused Joe. His eyes were narrowed, shrewd and hurt. "Tied up, huh? Still carrying the same old torch."

"The same—" Vaughn's eyes were wide.

"That Dran Hamilton character," said Joe tiredly, almost vindictively. He reached for the ring box. "Part two of the unholy trio—"

"Stop it!"

It was the first time he had seen her gentle violet eyes blazing. It was probably the first time they ever had. Then she picked up her gloves and said quietly, "I'd like to go now, Joe, if you don't mind."

"But—but Vaughn—what did I—I didn't mean any—"

"I know, I know," she said wearily. "Why, I haven't even thought about them for a long time. For too long. Perhaps I should have. I—*know* I should have. Joe, I have to go. I've got to get out of here. It's too small. Too many people, too many cheap little lights. I need some sun."

Almost frightened, he paid the check and followed her out. She was walking as if she were alone. He hesitated, then ran to catch up with her.

"It's a thing that you couldn't understand," she said dully when he drew alongside. She did not look up; for all he knew she may have been talking before he reached her. She went on, "There were three of us, and that's not supposed to be right. Twos, and twos, and twos, all through literature and the movies and the soap operas. This is something different. Or maybe it isn't different. Maybe it's wrong, maybe I'm too stupid to understand. . . . Joe, I'm sorry. Truly I am. I've been very selfish and unkind." There was that in her voice which stopped him. He stood on the pavement watching her move away. He shook his head, took one step, shook his head again, and then turned and plunged blindly back the way he had come.

* * *

"You're getting old," said Torth maliciously.

"Go away," said the other. "With two particles assimilated and the third about to be, matters have reached a critical point."

"There is nothing you could do about it no matter what happened," said Torth.

"Will you go away? What did you come for, anyway?"

"I was having an extrapolative session with another triad," Troth explained. "Subject: is the Eudiche experiment a hoax? Conclusion: it could be. Corollary: it might as well be, for all it has benefited our race. I came for your comments on that. You are an unpleasant and preoccupied entity, but for all that you are an authority."

The old one answered with angry evenness: "Answers: The Eudiche experiment is no hoax. It will benefit the race. As soon as Eudiche has perfected his fusion technique, we shall emigrate. Our crystalline casings are dust-motes to the bipeds of the third planet; our psychic existence will be all but unnoticeable to them until we synthesize. When we do, they will live for us, which is right and just. They will cease thinking their own thoughts, they will discontinue their single-minded activities. They will become fat and healthy and gracious as hosts."

"But observations indicate that they feed themselves largely by tilling the soil, that they combat the rigors of their climate by manufacturing artificial skins and complex dwelling shelters. If we should stop all that activity, they will die off, and we—"

"You always were a worrier, Torth," interrupted the other. "Know, then, that there are many of them and few of us. Each of us will occupy three of them, and those three will work together to keep themselves fed and us contented. The groups of three will be hidden in the mass of bipeds, having little or no physical contact with one another and remaining largely undetected. They will slaughter as they become hungry; after all, they are also flesh-eaters, and the reservoir of unoccupied bipeds will be large indeed. If, *after we get there, the bipeds never plant another seed nor build another dwelling, their own species will still supply an inexhaustible supply of food purely by existing to be slaughtered as needed. They breed fast and live long."*

Torth saluted the other. *"We are indeed entering upon an era of plenty. Your report is most encouraging. Our present hosts are small, few, and too easy to kill. I assume that the bipeds have somewhat the same miniscule intelligence?"*

"The bipeds of the third planet," said the other didactically, *"have mental powers several hundred times as powerful as do those we have dominated here. We can still take them*

over, of course, but it will be troublesome. Look at the length of time it is taking Eudiche. However, the reward is great. Once we have disrupted their group efforts by scattering our triads among them, I can predict an eternity of intriguing huntings and killings in order for our hosts to feed themselves. Between times, life will be a bountiful feast of their vital energies.

"Now, leave me, Torth. As soon as the final part of Eudiche's triad is settled in, we can expect the synthesis, by which he will come into full operation as an entity again. And that I want to observe. He has chosen well, and his three seeds are sprouting on fertile soil indeed."

"You have been uncharacteristically polite and helpful," conceded Torth. He left.

* * *

Dranley Hamilton drank the highball with the cold realization that it was one too many, and went on talking cleverly about his book. It was easy to do, because for him it was so easy to define what these fawning critics, publishers, clubwomen and hangers-on wanted him to say. He was a little disgusted with his book, himself, and with these people, and he was enjoying his disgust immensely, purely because he was aware of it and of his groundless sense of superiority.

Then there was a sudden, powerful agreement within him, compounded of noise, heat, stupidity and that last highball, which made him turn abruptly, to let a press-agent's schooled wisecrack spend itself on his shoulderblades as he elbowed his way through the room to the terrace doors. Outside, he stood with his arms on the parapet, looking out over the city and thinking, "Now, that didn't do me any good. I'm acting like something from the Village. Art for Art's sake. What's the matter with me anyway?"

There was a light step behind him. "Hello, Dranley Hamilton."

"Oh—it's you." He took in the russet hair, the blend of blendings which she used for a complexion. He had not noticed her before. "Do you know I have hung around this literary cackle-factory for the past two hours only because you were here and I wanted to get you alone?"

"Well!" said the girl. Then, with the same word in a totally different language, she added, "Well?"

He leaned back against the parapet and studied her tilted eyes. "No," he said finally. "No. I guess I was thinking of somebody else. Or maybe even something else."

Her real defenses went up in place of the party set. "Excuse *me!*" she said coldly.

"Oh, think nothing of it," he responded. He slapped her shoulder as if it were the withers of a friendly horse, and went back to the reception. *That was lousy,* he thought. *What's the matter with me?*

"Dran." It was Mike Pontif, from his publisher's publicity department. "You got that statement up about your next novel?"

"Next novel?" Dran looked at him thoughtfully. "There's not going to be a next novel. Not until I catch up on . . . something I should be doing instead." At the publicity man's bewildered expression, he added, "Going to bone up on biology."

"Oh," said the man, and winked. "Always kidding."

Dran was not kidding.

Manuel crumpled up the letter and hurled it into the corner of the communications shack. He shouldered through the door and went out on the beach, his boots thudding almost painfully down on the rough white coral sand. He drove his feet into the gritting stuff, stamping so that the heavy muscles of his thighs felt it. He scooped up the stripped backbone of a palm frond and cut at the wet sand by the water's edge as he walked, feeling the alternate pull of shoulders and chest.

He needed something. It wasn't women or liquor or people or solitude. It wasn't building or fighting or laughter. He didn't even need it badly. What he did want badly was to find out what this gentle, steady, omnipresent need was. He was sick of trying this and that to see if it would stop this infernal tugging.

He stopped and stared out to sea. The thick furrows across

his forehead deepened as he thought about the sea, and the way people wrote about it. It was always alive, or mysterious, or restless, or something. Why were people always hanging mysterious qualities on what should be commonplace? He was impatient with all that icky business.

"It's just wet salt and distance," he muttered. Then he spat, furious with himself, thinking how breathless the runt would be if she heard him say such a hunk of foolishness. He turned and strode back to the shack, feeling the sun too hot on the back of his neck, knowing he should have worn his helmet. He kicked open the screen door, blinked a moment against the indoor dimness, and went to the corner. He picked up the letter and smoothed it out.

> "From some remembered world
> We broke adrift
> Like lonely stars
> Divided at their birth.
>
> For some remembered dream
> We wait, and search
> With riven hearts
> A vast and alien earth . . ."

With the poem in his hand, Manuel glared around at useful things—the transmitter, the scrambler, the power supply. He looked at worthwhile things—the etched aluminum bracelets, the carved teak, the square-knotted belt he had made. And he looked at those other things, so meticulously machined, so costly in time and effort, so puzzling in function, that he had also made without knowing why. He shook the paper as if he wanted to hurt it. Why did she write such stuff? And why send it to him? What good was it?

He carried it to the desk, ripped out his personal file, and put it away. He filed it with Dran Hamilton's letters. He had no file for the runt's stuff.

When she concluded that she loved Dran, Vaughn wrote and said so, abruptly and with thoroughness. His answering telegram made her laugh and cry. It read:

NONSENSE, CHICKEN! ROMANTIC LOVE WRONG DIAGNOSIS. I JUDGE IT A CONVENTIONAL POETIC IMPULSE BETTER CONFINED TO PAPER. A CASE OF VERSE COME VERSE SERVED. TAKE A COLD SHOWER AND GO WRITE YOURSELF

A SONNET. BESIDES, WHAT ABOUT MANUEL? HE ARRIVES, INCIDENTALLY, NEW YEAR'S EVE AND INTENDS MEETING ME AT YOUR HOUSE. OKAY?

Dran arrived first, looking expensive and careless and, to Vaughn, completely enchanting. He bounded up the front steps, swung her off her feet and three times around before he kissed her, the way he used to do when they were children. For a long while they could say nothing but commonplaces, though their eyes had other things to suggest.

Dran leaned back in a kitchen chair as if it were a chaise longue and fitted a cigarette to a long ivory holder. "The holder?" he chattered. "Pure affectation. It does me good. Sometimes it makes me laugh at myself, which is healthy, and sometimes it makes me feel fastidious, which is harmless. You look wonderful with your hair down. Never pin it up or cut it again. Manuel's just turned down a commission. He ought to arrive about six, which gives us plenty of time to whirl the wordage. I liked your latest poems. I think I can help you get a collection published. The stuff's still too thin in the wrong places, though. So are you."

Vaughn turned down the gas under the percolator and set out cups. "You do look the successful young author. Oh, Dran, I'm *so* glad to see you!"

He took her hand, smiled up into her radiant face. "I'm glad too, chicken. You had me worried there for a while, with that love business."

Vaughn's eyes stopped seeing him for a moment. "I was —silly, I suppose," she whispered.

"Could be," he said cheerfully. "I'll tell you, hon—I like women. Without question there's a woman somewhere on earth that will make me go pitty-pat, quit drinking, write nothing but happy endings, and eat what's given to me instead of what I want. Maybe I've already met her and don't realize it. But one thing I'm sure of is that you're not that woman."

"What makes you so sure?"

"The same thing that makes you sure of it. You had a momentary lapse, it seems, but—come now; do you love me?"

"I wish Manuel would get here."

"Isn't that irrelevant?"

"No."

Then the coffee boiled over and the thread was lost.

They talked about Dran's book until Manuel arrived. The book was a strange one—one of those which captivates or infuriates, with no reader-reactions between the extremes. There were probably far more people who were annoyed by it than not, "which," said Dran, "is one of the few things the book has in common with its author."

"That remark," laughed Vaughn, "is the first you have made which sounded the way your picture in the *Literary Review* looked. It was awful. The decadent dilettante—the bored and viceful youth."

"It sells books," he said. "It's the only male answer to the busty book-jacket, or breast seller. I call it my frontispiece pose; separate but uplifted."

"And doubly false," snapped Vaughn. When he had quieted, she said, "but the book, Dran. There was one thing in there really worth mentioning—between us. The thing the critics liked the least."

"Oh—the dancer? Yes—they all said she was always present, never seen. Too little character for such a big influence."

"That's what I meant," said Vaughn. "I know and you know—and Manuel? We'll ask him—that the dancer wasn't a person at all, but an omnipresent idea, a pressure. Right?"

"Something like that cosmic search theme that keeps pushing you around in your work," he agreed. "I wonder what Manuel's counterpart is. It would have to be something he'd turn on a lathe."

Vaughn smiled. And then there was a heavy tread on the porch, the front door flew open, and the room was full of Manuel. "Hi, Dran. Where's the runt? Come out from under the furniture, you little—oh. There you are. Holy cow," he bellowed. "Holy sufferin' sepoys! You've shrunk!"

Dran threw up his hands. "Sepoys. Foreign background. Authentic touch."

Vaughn came forward and put out a demure hand. "I haven't shrunk, Manuel. It's you. You're thicker and wider than ever."

He took her hand, squeezed it, apologized when she yelped, rubbed his knuckles into her scalp until she yelped again, and threw himself onto the divan. "Lord, it's cold. Let's get going. Do something about this New Year's Eve and welcome home and stuff."

"Can't we just stay here and talk awhile?" asked Vaughn in rumpled petulance.

"What's the matter, runt?" Manuel asked in sudden concern, for Vaughn's eyes were filling.

Dran grinned. "I come in here, ice-cold and intellectual, and kiss the lass soundly. You come flying through the door, Lochinvar, shake hands with her and then proceed to roll her around like a puppy. Like the song says—try a little tenderness."

"You be quiet!" Vaughn almost shouted.

"Oh, so that's what you want." He strode across to Vaughn, brushed aside her protecting arms, and kissed her carefully in the exact center of the forehead. "Consider yourself smootched," he growled, "and we'll have no more of this lollygagging. Vaughn, you're acting like an abandoned woman."

Vaughn laced her anger with laughter as she said, "Abandoned is right. Now wait while I get my coat."

"I brought something back with me," Manuel said.

They were at a corner table at Enrique's, immersed in the privacy of noise, lights, and people. "What is it?" asked Vaughn. "Something special in costume jewelry?"

"Always want gilding, don't you, lily? Yes, I have the usual cargo. But that's not what I mean."

"Quell your greed," said Dran. "What is it, Manny?"

"It's a . . ." He swizzled his drink. "It's a machine. I don't know what it is."

"You don't—but what does it do? What's it made of?"

"Wire and a casting and a machined tube and ceramics, and I built it myself and I don't know what it does."

"I hate guessing games," said Dran petulantly.

Vaughn touched his arm, "Leave him alone, Dran. Can't you see he's bothered about it?" She turned quickly to the Marine, stroked the ribbons on his chest. "Talk about something else if you want to. What are these for?" she asked solicitously.

Manuel looked down at the ribbons, then thumbed the catch and removed them. He dropped them into Vaughn's hand. "For you," he said, his eyes glinting. "As a reward for talking like a hot damned civilian. I won't need 'em any more. My hitch is up; I'm out."

"Why, Manuel?"

"It's . . . I get—spells, sort of." He said it as if he were confessing to leprosy or even body odor. "Trances, like. Nobody knows about it. I wanted to get out from under before the brass wised up."

Vaughn, whose terror of "the ills our flesh is heir to" amounted to a neurosis, gasped and said, "Oh! What is it?

Are you sick? What do you think it is? Don't you think you ought to have an examination right away? Where does it hurt? Maybe it's a—"

Dran put an arm around her shoulders and his other hand firmly over her mouth. "Go on, Manny."

"Thanks, Dran. QRM, we call that kind of background noise in the Signal Corps. Shut up, short-change. About those spells . . . everything seems to sort of—recede, like. And then I work. I don't know what I'm doing, but my hands do. That's how I built this thing."

"What sort of a thing is it?"

Manuel scratched his glossy head. "Not a gun, exactly, but something like it. Sort of a solenoid, with a winding like nothing you ever dreamed of, and a condenser set-up to trigger it."

"A gun? What about projectiles?"

"I made some of those too. Hollow cylinders with a mechanical bursting arrangement."

"Filled with what?"

"Filled with nothing. I don't know what they're supposed to hold. Something composed of small particles, or a powder, or something. It wouldn't be an explosive, because there's this mechanical arrangement to scatter the stuff."

"Fuse?"

"Time," Manuel answered. "You can let her go now. I think she's stopped."

Dran said, "Manny, I've got the charge for your projectiles." He raised his hand a fraction of an inch. Vaughn said, "Let me *go!* Dran, let me go! Manuel, maybe you ate too much of that foreign—"

Dran's hand cut her off again.

Manuel said, "Like holding your hand over a faucet with a busted washer, isn't it?"

"More like getting a short circuit in a Klaxon. Vaughn, stop wriggling! Go on, Manny. I might as well tell you, something like it has happened to me. But I'll wait until you've finished. What about the fuse timing?"

"Acid vial. Double acting. There's an impact shield that pops up when a shell is fired, and a rod to be eaten through which starts a watch-movement. That goes for eight days. As for the acid—it'd have to be something really special to chew through that rod. Even good old Aqua Regia would take months to get through it."

"What acid are you using?"

Manuel shook his head. "That's one of the things I don't

know," he said unhappily. "That acid, and the charge, and most of all what the whole damned thing is for—those things I don't know."

"I think I've got your acid too," said Dran, shifting his hand a little because Vaughn showed signs of coming up for air. "But where are your specifications? What's the idea of making a rod so thick you can't find an acid to eat through it?"

Manuel threw up his hands. "*I* don't know, Dran. I know when it's right, that's all. I know before I rig my lathe or milling machine what I'm after." Hs face darkened, and his soft voice took on a tone of fury. "I'm sick and tired of getting pushed around. I'm tired of feeling things I can't put a name to. For the first time in my life I can't whip something or get away from it."

"Well, what are you going to do?"

"What *can* I do? Get out of the service, hole up somewhere, finish this work."

"How do you know it won't go on for the rest of your life?"

"I don't know. But I know this. I know what I've done is done right, and that when it's finished, that'll be the end of it," said Manuel positively. "Hey—you better turn her loose. The purple face goes great with the hair, but it's beginning to turn black."

Dran released Vaughn, and just then the bells began to ring.

* * *

"Old one—"
The other turned on Torth. "Get out. Get out and leave me alone. Get out!"
Torth got.

* * *

The bells. . . .

"Not now," smiled Vaughn. "Not now. I'll give you rascals the punishment you deserve next year sometime." She reached out her arms, and they came close to her. She kissed Manuel, then Dran, and said, "Happy New Year, darlings."

The bells were ringing, and the city spoke with a mighty voice, part hum, part roar, part whistle, part scream, all a unison of joy and hope. *"Should auld acHappy-Nooooo*

Yearzhz-z-zh-h-h . . ." said the city, and Manuel pulled Vaughn closer (and Dran with her, because Dran was so close to her) and Manuel said, "This is it. This is right, the three of us. I quit. Whether I like it or not don't matter. I got it and I'm stuck with it. I . . ."

EUDICHE!

No one said that. No one shouted it out, but for a split second there was a gasping silence in the club, in the floors above and the floors below, as three abstracts coalesced and a great subetheric emanation took place. It was more joyous than all the joy in the city, and a greater voice than that of all the other voices; and it left in a great wave and went rocketing out to the stars. And then someone started to sing again, and the old song shook the buildings.

"*. . . and never brought to mind . . .*"

* * *

"*It's done!*" said the old one.

Torth replied caustically. "I appreciate the news. You realize that not one of us on Titan could have missed that signal."

"*Eudiche has succeeded,*" *exulted the old one. "A new era for our race . . . on his next transmission we will start the emigration.*"

"*And you had doubts of Eudiche.*"

"*I did—I did. I admit it. But it is of no moment now—he has overcome his defection.*"

"*What is it, this defection?*"

"*Stop your ceaseless questions and leave me to my joy!*"

"*Tell me that, decrepit one, and I shall go.*"

"*Very well, Eudiche was imbalanced. He suffered from an overbroadening of the extrapolative faculty. We call it empathy. It need not concern you. It is an alien concept and a strange disease indeed.*"

* * *

Eudiche left, still in three parts, but now one. He stopped at the railroad station for a heavy foot-locker, and at a hotel for a large suitcase. And in the long ride in a taxi, Eudiche thought things out—not piecemeal, not single-mindedly in each single field, but with the magnificent interaction of a multiple mind.

"Is it certain that everything will fit together?" asked the mechanical factor.

"It certainly should. The motivation was the same, the drive was almost identical, and the ability in each case was of a high order," said the intellectual.

The aesthetic was quiet, performing its function of matching and balancing.

The mechanical segment had a complimentary thought for the intellectual. "That spore chest is a mechanical miracle for this planet. Wasn't it gruelling, without a full mechanical aptitude to help?"

"The bipeds have wide resources. Once the design is clear, they can make almost anything. The spores themselves have started lines of research on molds, by the way, that will have far-reaching effects."

"And good ones," murmured the aesthetic. "Good ones."

Far away from the city Eudiche paid the driver and the intellectual told him to come back in the morning. And then Eudiche struck off through the icy fields, across a frozen brook, and up a starlit slope, carrying with him the spore case, the projector, and the projectiles.

It was cold and clear, and the stars competed with one another—and helped one another, too, the aesthetic pointed out: ". . . for every star which can't outshine the others seems to get behind and help another one be bright."

Eudiche worked swiftly and carefully and set up the projector. The spores were loaded into the projectiles, and the projectiles were primed with the acid and set into the gun.

The aesthetic stood apart with the stars, while the mechanical and the intellectual of Eudiche checked the orbital computations and trained the projector. It was exacting work, but there was not a single wasted motion.

The triggering was left to charge for a while, and Eudiche rested. The aesthetic put a hand to the projector—that seeking hand, always, with her, a gesture of earnestness.

"Back to Titan, and may the race multiply and grow great," she intoned. "Search the spaces between the stars and find Titan's path; burst and scatter your blessings at his feet."

The condensers drank and drank until they had their fill and a little over—

Phup! It was like the popping of a cork. Far up, seemingly among the stars, there was a faint golden streak, gone instantly.

"Reload," said the intellectual.

Two worked; the third, by her presence, guided and balanced and added proportion to each thought, each directive effort. Eudiche waited, presently, for the projector to charge again. "Earth . . ." crooned the aesthetic. "Rich, wide, wonderful earth, rich with true riches, rich in its demonstrations of waste . . . wealthy earth, which can afford to squander thousands upon thousands of square miles in bleak hills on which nothing grows . . . wealthy earth with its sea-sunk acres, its wandering rivers which curiously seek everything of interest, back and forth, back and backwards and seaward again, seeking in the flatlands. And for all its waste it produces magnificently, and magnificently its products are used. Humans are its products, and through the eyes of humans are seen worlds beyond worlds . . . in the dreams of the dullest human are images unimaginable to other species. Through their eyes pour shapes and colors and a hungry hope that has no precedent in the cosmos."

"Empathy," defined the intellectual: "The ability to see through another's eyes, to feel with his finger-tips.

"To know fire as the feathers of a Phoenix know it. To know, as a bedded stone, the coolth of brook-water . . ."

Phup!

"Reload," said the intellectual.

In its time the second projectile followed, and then a third and a fourth.

* * *

"This is the machine," old Torth said to the youngster. "It was monopolized, long ago, by a caustic old triad who has since died. And may I join him soon, for it troubles me to be so old."

"And what was the machine for?"

"One Eudiche was analyzed into his three components and sent to that star there."

"It's a planet."

"Youth knows too much, too young," grumbled Torth.

"And why was Eudiche sent?"

"To test the sending; to synthesize himself there; and to prepare for mass emigration of our kind to the planet."

"He failed?"

"He failed. He took over three inhabitants successfully enough, but that was all. He had empathy, you know."

The youngster shuddered. "No loss."

"No loss," repeated Torth. "And then the reason for invasion was removed, and no one bothered to use the machine again, and no one will."

"That was when the molds came?"

"Yes, the molds. Just as we came out of space so long ago, as crystalline spores, so these molds arrived on Titan. At that time, you know, we possessed all Titans and reproduced faster than they did. We had to expand."

"It is not so now," said the youngster with confidence.

"No," said Torth. *"Happily, no. The products of the molds —and the molds grow profusely here—worked miracles with the metabolism of our hosts. They reproduce faster and they live longer."*

"And will they never overpopulate Titan?"

"Not in our time, not in any predictable time. Titan can support billions of the little creatures, and there are only a few thousand today. The rate of increase is not that great. Just great enough to give us, who are parasites, sufficient hosts."

"And—what happened to Eudiche?"

*   *   *

"He died," said Vaughn. Her voice was shocked, distraught in the cold dawn.

"He had to die," said Dran sorrowfully. "His synthesis was complete in us three. His consistency was as complete. His recognition of the right to live gave him no alternative. He saved his own race on its own terms, and saved—spared, rather—spared us on human terms. He found what we were, and he loved it. Had he stayed here, he and his progeny and his kind would have destroyed the thing he loved. So he died."

The grey light warmed as they started down the hill, and then the dawn came crashing up in one great crescendo of color, obliterating its pink prelude and establishing the theme for the sun's gaudy entrance. Drunk with its light, three people crossed the frozen brook and came to the edge of the road.

At last Manuel spoke. "What have we got here?"

Dran looked at the satchels, at Vaughn, at Manuel. "What have you got?"

Manuel kicked his foot locker. "I've got the beginnings of a space drive. You've got a whole new direction in biological chemistry. Runt— Oh my god, will you look at that face. I know—poems."

"Poems," she whispered, and smiled. The dawn had not been like that smile.

The taxi came. They loaded their cases in and sat very close together in the back.

"No one of us will ever be greater than any other," Dran said after a time. "We three have a life, not lives. I don't know anything yet about the details of our living, except that they will violate nothing."

Vaughn looked into Manuel's face, and into Dran's. Then she chuckled, "Which means I'll probably marry Joe."

They were very close. Dran again broke the silence. "My next book will be my best. It will have this dedication:

"What Vaughn inspires, I design, and Manuel builds."

And so it came about.

Poor Joe.

This odd little thing—actually one of the first stories I ever wrote in my life—was bought by Ray Palmer. I met Ray many years ago, on my first trip to Chicago, and was immensely impressed. He made a smashing success of the old Amazing Stories, *and then put over, in its pages, one of the most . . . well, amazing ploys ever to hit the public press. To this day fights start in bars over the "Shaver Mystery" or the "Shaver Hoax", depending upon who's swinging at the moment. There is as much documentation that Ray believed in the Shaver affair as that he didn't, and I for one don't much care: true or not, it was a colorful and kooky piece of business and I enjoyed every minute of it and all the arguments. If the reader is unfamiliar with it, I suggest he look it up. Any s-f fan will point the way. If it doesn't stimulate your sense of wonder it will stimulate your sense of outrage.*

I'd like to pay one sober tribute to Ray, absolutely aside from the foregoing: he is one of the most courageous human beings who ever lived.

The Heart

I DON'T LIKE to be poked repeatedly by a hard bony fore-finger until I give my attention to its owner, particularly if said owner is a very persistent drunk who has been told to scram twice and still hasn't got the idea. But this drunk was a woman, and I couldn't bring myself to slug her, somehow.

"Please, mister," she droned. I pulled my sleeve out of her fingers. The movement was reflex, the involuntary recoil at the sight of a dead face.

She needed a drink; a fact that made little difference to me. So did I. But I had only enough change to take care of my own wants, and nobody ever had a chance to call me Sir Galahad. "What the hell do you want?"

She didn't like to be snapped at like that. She almost told

me off; but the thought of a free drink made her change her mind. She had a bad case of shakes. She said, "I want to talk to you, that's all."

"What about?"

"Somebody told me you write stuff. I got a story for you."

I sighed. Some day, maybe, I would be released from people who said a) "Where do you get your ideas?" and people who said b) "You want a story? My life would make the swellest—"

"Babe," I said, "I wouldn't put you on paper if you were Mata Hari. Go scare someone else with that phiz of yours, and leave me alone."

Her lips curled back wickedly from her teeth, and her eyes slitted; and then, with shocking suddenness, her face relaxed completely. She said, "I'd hate you if I wasn't afraid to hate anything ever again."

In that second I was deathly afraid of her, and that in itself was enough to get me interested. I caught her shoulder as she turned away, held up two fingers to the barkeep, and steered her to a table. "That last crack of yours is worth a drink," I said.

She was grateful. "One drink," she said, "and I'm paid in full. In advance. You want the story?"

"No," I said, "But go ahead." She did.

I always kept pretty much to myself. I didn't have the looks that other women have, and to tell the truth, I got along fine without them. I had a fair enough job, slapping a typewriter for the county coroner, and I had a room big enough for me and a few thousand books. I ran to seed a little, I guess. Ah—never mind the buildup. There's a million like me, buried away in dusty little offices. We do our work and keep our mouths shut and nobody gives much of a damn about us, and we don't mind it.

Only something happened to me. I was coming out of the borough hall one afternoon when I ran into a man. He was thin and sallow, and when I bumped him he folded up, gasping like a fish. I caught him and held him up. He couldn't have weighed more than about ninety-four. He hung onto me for a minute and then he was all right. Grinned at me. Said, "Sorry, miss. I got used to a bad heart quite some time ago, but I wish it wouldn't get in other people's way."

I liked his attitude. A pump like that, and he wasn't crying any. "Keep your chin up that high and it won't get in anyone's way," I told him. He tipped his hat and went on, and I felt good about it all evening.

I met him a couple of days later, and we talked for a minute. His name was Bill Llanyn. Funny Welsh name. After a few weeks it didn't sound funny any more, I'd like to have had it for my own. Yes, it was that way. We had practically everything in common except that I have a constitution like a rhinoceros. Had then, anyway. He had a rotten little job as assistant curator in a two-for-a-nickel museum. Fed the snakes and tarantulas in the live-animal corner. He only got cigarette money out of it, but managed to eat on his wages because he couldn't smoke. I knocked together a supper one evening in my place. He went mad over my books. It was all I could do to pry him loose. Oh, the poor man! It used to take him ten minutes to get up the one flight of stairs to my room. No, he was no Tarzan.

But I—loved that little man.

That was something I thought I didn't know how to do. I—well, I'm not going to talk about it. I'm telling you a story: right? Well, it's not a love story. Mind if I finish your drink, too? I—

Well, I wanted to marry him. You might think it would be a joke of a marriage. But God, all I wanted was to have him around, maybe even see him happy for once in his life. I knew I'd outlast him, but I didn't think about that. I wanted to marry him and be good to him and do things for him, and when he got his call, he wouldn't be all alone to face it.

It wasn't much to ask—oh yes—I had to do the asking. He wouldn't—but he wasn't having any. He sat on my armchair in front of the fire with an ivory-bound copy of Goethe in one hand, and held up his fingers one by one as he counted off his reasons why not. He wasn't making enough money to support both of us. He was liable to drop dead any second. He was too much of a wreck for any woman to call husband. He said he loved me, but he loved me too much to hang himself around my neck. Said I should find myself a real live man to get married to. Then he got up, put on his hat, said, "I'll get out now. I never loved anyone before. I'm glad I do now. You won't see me again. I haven't got much longer to be around; I'd just as soon you never knew just when I check out. That's the only thing left in the world that I can do for you." Then he came over to me and said some more, and be damned to you; that's for me to remember and for you to think about. But after he left I never saw him again.

I tried to get back into the old routine of typing and books, but it was rough. I did a lot of reading, trying to forget about it, trying to forget Bill Llanyn's wasted face. But everything I read seemed to be about him. Guess I picked the wrong stuff. Schopenhauer. Poe. Dante. Faulkner. My mind went round and round. I knew I'd feel better if I had something to hate.

Hate's a funny thing. I hope you don't ever know how— how *big* it can be. Use it right, and it's the most totally destructive thing in the universe. When I realized that, my mind stopped going round and round in those small circles, and it began to drive straight ahead. I got it all clear in my mind. Listen now—let me tell you what happened when I got going.

I found something to hate. Bill Llanyn's heart—the ruined, inefficient organ that was keeping us apart. No one can ever know the crazy concentration I put into it. No one has ever lived to describe the *solidness* of hate when it begins to form into something real. I needed a miracle to make over Bill's heart, and in hate I had a power to work it. My hate reached a greatness that nothing could withstand. I knew it just as surely as a murderer knows what he has done when he feels his knife sink into his victim's flesh. But I was no murderer. Death wasn't my purpose. I wanted my hatred to reach into his heart, sear out what was bad and let him take care of the rest. I was doing what no one else has ever done— hating constructively. If I hadn't been so insanely anxious to put my idea to work, I would have remembered that hate can build nothing that is not evil, cause nothing that is not evil.

Yes, I failed. My boss came into the office one afternoon last week with a sheaf of morgue notes for me to type in triplicate and file away. Post mortems on stiffs that had been picked up during the last forty-eight hours. William Llanyn was there. Cause of death, heart failure. I stared at the notes for a long time. The coroner was standing looking out of the window. Noticed my typewriter stop without starting again, I guess. Without turning around, he said.

"If you're looking at those heart-failure notes, don't ask me if there isn't some more to it—pericarditis, mitral trouble, or anything. Just write 'heart failure.' "

I asked why. He said, "I'll tell you, but damned if I'll go on the record with a thing like that. The man didn't have any heart at all."

The woman got up and looked at the clock.

"Where you headed?" I asked.

"I'm catching a train out of here," she said. She went to the door. I said goodnight to her on the sidewalk. She went down toward the station. I headed uptown. When the police emergency wagon screamed by me a few minutes later I didn't have to go down to the tracks to see what had happened.

THE INCUBI OF PARALLEL X is the most horrible title to appear over my byline, and I'm sure Malcolm Reiss, the editor, will forgive me for saying so. It was a typical Planet Stories title, and I've been sitting here trying to remember some of the parody titles George O. Smith used to dream up. I can, too, but I can't share them with you, not even in these liberated days. . . .

I haven't seen Mal in many years, but we've corresponded; he is hale and hearty and hard at work in New York. He is one of the first discoverers of Ray Bradbury; I have a letter from Ray in which he describes an act of Mal Reiss's which bears out the nicest of the nice things I have said about editors in my introduction: he once turned down a Bradbury story because he knew it would sell to a major magazine, and it did. I have one other clear recollection of Mal Reiss: Teeth. Aside from Ray Bradbury he has the most brilliant teeth I have ever seen. I bet when they were in the same room together, and smiled, any third party would get snowblind.

The Incubi of Parallel X

IT'S SMALLER, Garth thought as he lay on his belly on top of the hill and looked down, through carefully parted branches, at Gesell Hall. The Hall had towered over him when he was a child, last year, last week, last night, in his dreams. And now, at the moment he had schooled himself for, waited for since the day his world had ended, he could feel no thrill, no triumph—only it's smaller.

The great building, with its rambling wings, its twisted, broken power receptor antennae, its yellow weed-grown courts, lay as if in the hollow of some mighty neck, with a cliff and a mountain shoulder shrugging it into its crowded, cluttered, sheltered state.

I should have known, he thought. I was only a kid when I left—when the Ffanx—

He lost himself in the restimulated dream, the clear mental picture of his toy spaceship, hovering in midair on a

110

pillar of koolflame fire, and his child's dream of worlds, and then the shrill thunder of jets—real jets, Ffanx jets— which had brought an end to his dream and his childhood and his world.

Garth Gesell slipped a long-fingered hand under his abdomen and hauled out a knobby root which rowelled him. *It was there,* he thought, *right there by the main building. The Ffanx came, and I ran around to the front and through the double doors, and right in to Dad and Mooley. And the roof came down, and Mooley the cat, ran through fire and was naked and agonized, and then there was Dad's head with a splinter through the bridge of his nose and the end of it in a ruined eye, talking to me . . . `talking out of a mountain of rubble, out of torture, out of gentleness and greatness, asking me to save a race and a world and a system . . .*

Well, he was back. Not back home, for this was enemy territory now. All the backslid, savage world was enemy territory for anyone who ventured out of his settlement, and Garth's adopted village was many a long day's march behind him. Behind him, too, were years of growth and training and of living with the nagging, driving force of his childhood promise to his father: I shall open the Gateway.

"I shall open the Gateway." He said it aloud, intensely, in a deep re-dedication to his father's wish. And then he threw himself violently to one side.

His watchful subsconscious, his trained hearing, were a shade too slow to avoid the blow completely. The short, stubby spear whacked him painfully between the shoulder-blades instead of burying itself in his back. He rolled back over it, snatching it up as he rolled, and bounced to his feet in a single fluid motion, striking upward with the spear. He got a quick impression of a tall, wide, golden figure which, without moving its feet, bent gracefully aside to avoid the spear's hungry point. Then there was a sharp blow on Garth's wrist and the spear went flying end over end into the undergrowth.

Garth stood, shaken and helpless, grasping his wrist, and looked up into the easy smile of the stranger.

"Move fast, don't you?" said the man. He had a broad, clean-cut face and the rasping, rapid speech of a Northerner. He stood with his thick legs apart, the knees slightly flexed. Garth had the impression that from that stance the man could move instantly in any direction, including straight up. "But not fast enough for Bronze," the man added.

Garth understood the name and the reason for it—the

golden skin and yellow hair, the rivet-studded belt and boots were obviously a personal trade-mark. In his hand Bronze held a polished throwing-stick, the source of the stubby, bullet-like spear. He slowly whacked the end of it into a wide, horny palm as he studied Garth. "What are you after?"

Garth thumbed over his shoulder at the crumbling building down in the green hollow. "What do you call that place?"

"Gesell."

"I am Gesell too."

Bronze's face turned into a mask. He stepped past Garth, dropping his throwing-stick into the quiver of spears which hung behind his right shoulder. He stooped and picked up Garth's weapon and handed it back to him.

Garth carefully avoided saying "Thanks."

"I heard you say you'd open the Gateway."

Garth nodded.

Bronze said, "Could I help you?" and in that moment Garth knew he'd won. He suppressed a smile. "I don't need help," he said.

"You might," said Bronze.

Garth shrugged as if he didn't care. In reality, he cared a great deal. He had known for a long time that he'd have to recruit some help, and he liked the looks of those big shoulders, and of the obvious skill that had gone into the man's trappings and weapons. "What's it to you if I open the Gateway?"

Bronze licked his lips. Then, with no attempt to conceal his motives, he said, "There's women in there. Thousands of 'em. The best, the smartest on this world or off it." He paused. "I come here all the time. I sit up here and look down at the Hall and try to figure a way in." He spread his big hands. "If you were trying to stop me from getting to those women, I wanted to kill you. If you can help me get to them, I'm on your side. All the way. See?"

"Fair enough," said Garth, and let the grin come through this time. "Not enough women around here for you?"

"Not enough women in the whole damn world. Seven in Prellton—that's my village—and a hundred men. Over the hill there, in Haddon Town, there's twice as many women and three times as many men."

"So you want the Gateway open so you can cut loose with the whole lot of 'em?"

"Me?" cried Bronze. "No, man, I just want one. Just one woman, all for me."

"I see you're a reasonable man," said Garth smiling. "You can go with me."

Bronze looked as if Garth had given him a kingdom, and a pair of wings to boot. "I heard of you Gesells."

"You heard of my father," said Garth.

"They still tell stories about him."

If there has to be a shrine, there's bound to be a legend, thought Garth. "Why didn't you try breaking into the Hall?"

"Some tried, one time or another," said Bronze. He cast a quick, fearful glance down into the hollow. "They're all dead."

"That's what I heard." Garth studied Bronze thoughtfully. "Ever see it happen?"

"Once." Bronze swung his spear quiver off his shoulder and squatted on the bank, running the spears nervously through his thick fingers as he spoke, testing their points, their grooved hafts. "I was to watch, me and Rob O'Bennet and his fighting-boys. Flan of Haddon's Town and his men got the main assault because they have the larger settlement. We were to storm down and back them once they'd breached the Hall." He paused and wet his lips. His amber eyes were haunted. "Two Guardians the Hall had, then as now—two only, just two against the two hundred of us. Flan's boys raised a yell you could hear over the mountain, and charged. Not a sign of life from the Hall until they were half across the court there—" he pointed— "and then the Guardians stepped out, one from the north corner, one from the south, by the little door. There was a blast of green fire the like of which words won't handle." Bronze covered his eyes as he spoke. "I saw it stretch between the two Guardians for a half second, and then I was dazzle-blinded.

"When I could see again my brave boys were gone, leaving me writhing my burned eyes into the grass here. And down there in the court lay Flan and thirty-eight of his boys, smoking and black."

He paused while the terrifying picture died behind his eyes. "Afterward," he said, "a party of us went over to Haddon's Town to see if so many dead hadn't left a widow for us, but they had the place well stockaded."

Garth made no comment. "Tell me what you know of the Guardians."

"I'll tell you little enough," said Bronze. "But if I said what I'd heard I'd be talking a month or more. All you ever see of them is that pointed cowl and the long habit that goes to the ground. Some say they're men and women—or were.

Some say they're monsters from the other side of the Gateway."

"We'll soon see," said Garth.

"You're a Gesell," said Bronze, his voice hoarse with suppressed excitement. "You can just walk in like a guest."

"I can not," said Garth shortly. "I hate to disappoint you, Bronze, but a lot of water has gone over the dam since the Ffanx conquered us. My father built the Gateway twenty years ago, thinking that it would guard those women for the month or so it took to smash the Ffanx. They killed my father and closed the Gateway. And by then the world was a ruin, with the women gone and the men fighting over the handful who were left, and the secret of the Gateway locked up in the brain of an eight-year-old child. And now the Hall is a shrine, and the guards are Guardians, science is magic and each part of the world fights every other part."

"What are you saying? You can't just walk in, and you a Gesell?"

"Everything's changed," said Garth patiently. "I've listened to every traveler's tale, read every record—there are damned few enough—and it all comes to the one stupidity: I am the only man alive who can open the Gateway, and those dedicated fools down there will kill me on sight if I go near it."

"How do I know you're a Gesell?" said Bronze, in reawakened suspicion.

"You don't," said Garth. Without looking up or turning, he made one sudden, brief movement. The tube seemed to leap from his right holster into his hand. "Look, Bronze."

Bronze's face went stony. "What is it? What is that thing?"

Garth pressed the stud on the side of the tube. A beam of light leaped from the tube to bathe Bronze's terrified face. The big man cried out, and then sat frozen, eyes shut in terror. Garth turned it off and dropped it back into the holster. "My name is Gesell," he said conversationally, "but I don't give a hub-forted damn if you believe it or not."

"What was it? What did it do? That light, that white light—"

"Just light," said Garth, and laughed. He slapped the big man on his meaty shoulder. "Stop your chattering."

"You shouldn't 'a done that," said Bronze hoarsely. "You didn't have to scare me like that, Gesell. I said I'd help. I wasn't backing out. I believe you."

"Good. Now shut up and let me figure this out."

They stood at the crest of a wooded slope that fell away almost vertically to the clearing below. The Hall stood in the center of the clearing, and beyond it was another rise— the mountain shoulder itself, not quite as high as the elevation on which they hid. The weed-grown court offered no shelter except a couple of giant trees, one of which towered over the central building. One thick branch held a mighty, protective arm over the low roof. Garth stared at it and at the opposite slope.

"Bronze!"

Bronze was by him, almost crowding him in his eagerness to serve. "What, Gesell?"

"Just how good are you with that womera of yours?"

"Good enough, Gesell. I once killed a deer at ninety yards."

"How many?"

"Seventy," said Bronze, finding himself fixed by Garth's deep eyes. He gulped and grinned.

"It's damn near a hundred and fifty over to the top of the bluff—see it there, the sheer rock straight over the Hall?"

"Uh-huh. I could peg a spear over there. Wouldn't hit too hard, though."

"Could you put it exactly there?"

Confidently Bronze made a ring of his thumb and forefinger. "I could put it through that."

"Show me."

Bronze selected a spear and fitted the butt of it to the cup-shaped hook in the end of his throwing stick. He tested the ground under his feet, glanced overhead to check for overhanging brush, and moved a little to the left. For a moment he stood poised, fixing the opposite cliff with a hypnotic eye. Then he moved. His arm was a blur, and the stick itself was invisible. It all but crackled as it cleft the air.

For a brief moment Garth lost sight of the spear altogether. Then his quick eye caught its flicker just before it stopped, deep-buried in a tree-trunk at the lip of the rock cliff. He held his breath, and in a second or so he heard, through the warm afternoon air, the soft, solid *thunk* of its impact.

Incredible! He thought. He said, boredly, "Not too bad. I'd hate to depend on that thing if there was any wind, though."

Garth threw off his belt. He stood up in a single garment, a skin-tight shorts-and-tunic combination of midnight blue, with a narrow white stripe all the way around under his armpits and another just below his waistline. Raising his arms, he felt along this line and drew out a small ring, which he slid along the stripe. It was, judging by the wide eyes and slack mouth, Bronze's first view of a slide fastener.

Garth repeated the movement with a second ring on the lower stripe, and drew off the center portion of his tunic over his head—a single, resilient tube of soft, thin fabric. He ran its edge through his fingers, stopped, and carefully picked out a thread, which he worked free. Ignoring the astounded Bronze, he began to unravel the material.

"What you doing?"

Garth said, "Make yourself useful. I want you to sweep the ground clean—really clean—some place where it's solid. I want an area six by six feet without so much as a straw on it, with clear air above it. Get to it."

Willing and mystified, Bronze did as he was told. By the time Garth had thirty feet of thread cleared, the area was ready and Bronze, panting, was back at Garth's side. Garth took pity on him—he was obviously about to burst with curiosity. He held up the thread. "Break off a piece for me, Bronze boy."

Bronze took the end of the thread, wrapped it around his fists, and—"Wait!" laughed Garth.

He picked up two heavy pieces of tree-branch, unwound the thread from the big unresisting fists, and took a couple of turns of the thread around each piece of wood, leaving about six inches of thread between them. "Now try it," he said. "Grip the wood, not the thread."

Puzzled, Bronze grasped the two pieces of wood and pulled. The thread went taut with a musical twang which rose in pitch as Bronze pulled. A look of utter amazement crossed his broad face. He relaxed, turned the two pieces of wood so that he wound up more thread and had only two inches between them. He set his back against a tree, knotted his jaw, and, with his great hands close to his chest, began to pull. His triceps swelled until the stretched skin shone. His body moved visibly away from the tree that he leaned against as his scapular muscles bunched and crawled.

There was a muffled crackling from his shoulders, and Garth stepped forward in alarm. Then one of the pieces of wood gave. The thread sliced through it like a scythe through a stand of wheat, and Bronze stood gasping, staring foolishly at the cleancut stub of branch in his hand. The thread fell away, unstretched, unbroken.

"I gave you the wood," Garth grinned, "because it would've sliced through your paws."

"What Ffanx stuff is that?" gasped Bronze.

"That isn't Ffanx stuff; it's strictly human. Molecularly condensed fibre spun under massive ion bombardment, if that makes any never mind to you. It has linear cohesion in the order of six tons test and eight and a half tons breaking strain. And it has no rotary cohesion at all."

"Yeah," said Bronze, "but what is it?"

"It's what you're going to tie to a spear and fire over the gulch for me. Now let's get busy and flake it out here. There's four hundred yards of it in this shirt. Half that should be enough. We'll give it a little more."

For two hours, as the afternoon shadows grew long, they worked, laying the thread meticulously in a series of small coils. Each turn of each coil lay flat and obedient. Slowly the coils began to carpet the cleared area. They talked little, except toward the end of the laborious job. Finally—"That should do it," Garth said.

Bronze straightened up and punched himself in his aching kidneys. "I'm hungry."

"Feed us," said Garth.

Bronze took up his quiver and throwing-stick without a word, and glided away through the underbrush. Within a quarter of an hour he was back, carrying two large rabbits. One had a ragged hole through the head just behind the eyes, and the other was still impaled through the ribcage and heart by one of the stubby spears. Bronze squatted down, pulled out a worn knife, and with the swift casualness of long practice, gutted and skinned one of the animals and handed the warm and dripping quarters to Garth.

"Now listen to me," Garth said with his mouth full. "I don't know for sure who those Guardians are. But this I do know for sure—that green fire you saw doesn't come from them. It comes from under the ground—an energy field activated by something they carry under those long robes . . . Why do I bother to explain anything to you?"

"I'm listening," grunted Bronze, spitting out a piece of gristle.

"All right. Now get this, it takes two Guardians, both on the line of those underground cables, to set off that fire. But *it takes two of them to do it.* Do you understand? If I can get one of them out of the way, you can jump the other one without any danger."

"Uh?" Bronze wiped rabbit blood off his chin.

"Are you following this? I'm going to leave you in a minute, and I want to know I can depend on you. Are you going to take my word for it—that you can tackle a Guardian without danger of getting burned?"

Bronze looked at him. "You said I could, didn't you?" he asked simply.

Garth let the grin come through again. "I think we're going to make it, Bronze boy," he said. "Now here's the plan."

The night was cool and still, but Garth, naked except for his belt, his boots, and the briefest of shorts—which were all that was left of his tunic—was warm and slick with sweat as he completed the long, silent climb to the top of the bluff. He filled and emptied his lungs in deep, open-throated gasps as he felt his way along the lip of the sheer rock wall of the cliff. He found the bald spot and the tree into which Bronze had sunk his test spear that afternoon.

He stepped behind the tree in which Bronze's spear still stuck, and, reaching around it with his flashlight in his hand, sent a quick, white beam up the trunk.

Then he waited.

There was a crescent moon in the sky, a chunky moon that urgently wanted to be gibbous. Somewhere a katydid cried for the grease like the proverbial squeaky wheel, and a tree-toad plucked away at its piano-wire heartstrings. Over the brink was blackness—eighty feet or better, straight down—and then, away from the cliff's shadow, a hundred yards from the base of the bluff, stood the arched shadow of the great tree with its limb stretched out over the main building like a giant frozen in a gesture of benison.

Where was Bronze? The opposite hill was a featureless mass of shadow and shifting moonlight. Was he there, sighting carefully on the place where he had seen Garth's gleam of light? Or was he gone, freed from the spell of wonderment and awe that Garth had put on him, strolling back toward his village to spend tonight and the rest of his muscle-bound life with idle speculation about the time he almost helped to open the Gateway?

The katydid and the treefrog suddenly were more than Garth could bear. With a snort of impatience he stepped from behind the tree. Immediately there was a whining whisper that crescendoed closer—air fanned his nose and eyes, and something slammed into the tree trunk. He went to his knees, staring up into blackness and then, in spite of himself, laughed. "I hope I've used up all my dumbness for tonight," he thought ruefully. He had known the impossibility of Bronze's hitting the tree again, especially in the dark—and had almost stepped out of the shelter of the tree-trunk in time to catch the spear with his silly head.

The spear hadn't stuck in the tree, for he had cautioned Bronze to bury the point in a piece of heartwood; he'd never have been able to pull it out of the tree, and, to do what he had to do, the thread-end must be free.

He fumbled about for the spear and found it. From his belt-pouch he drew a pair of molded gloves, thin, light, impenetrable, made of the same condensed matter as his tunic. Slipping them on, he picked up the spear and purely by touch found the thread. He brought it in hand over hand, yards of it, until suddenly it jerked sharply, twice, in his grip. He grinned. That was Bronze's "Good luck!"

Taking a bight of the thread, he walked once around the tree, thrust the loop of the bight under the main part where it would be pinched between that part and the tree-trunk. A slight tug on the free end would cast the line adrift.

He took a deep breath and walked to the cliff-edge. Everything depended on his estimates of the distances involved.

This is it, he thought. Carefully he took the thread at the point his measurements had brought him to, and tied it to the back of his belt. He knelt and swept a space on the ground, and carefully recoiled the line so it would flake away freely. Then he went to the edge of the cliff, reached up over his head, and got his gloved hands on the anchored part of the line, where it passed tautly from tree to tree across the hollow. He watched then, and tried not to think.

The buildings were dark, except for a dim orange light in the main Hall. He could see a flickering, an occasional movement as if restless figures inside passed and re-passed the light.

What the hell was Bronze doing over there? Had he forgotten what he was supposed to do next? The big, stupid, slow . . .

From the other side of the canyon came a titanic crashing as a boulder went bounding down the slope, and with it a blood-chilling yell that echoed and re-echoed and faded repetitively off into the distance. It sounded like a score of lost souls calling and answering from strategic points up and down both sides of the valley.

What a set of pipes! Garth thought, and stepped off the cliff.

He could feel the rod-hard, stretched thread humming in his

hands as the gentle night wind stroked it. He hung for a moment, then put one hand before the other. And again. And again. His body began to swing forward and back as he went along the line. He swore under his breath and checked the movement by a swift, synchronized run-and-stop, run-and-stop with his hands.

His shoulders began to ache and he tried to forget it. He hung by one hand for a moment and allowed himself the luxury of bringing the other arm down, flexing the fingers. Hand over hand over hand over hand . . .

He put his hands together and crossed the wrists, so that his body turned to look back the way he had come. The shadowed cliff he had left was already distant, one with the hill-blackness that surrounded the buildings. He went on. Before and below him, the great tree came closer and closer and closer as he inched along. Too close?

He swung along, arms all but numb, shoulders an agony, hands reduced to two stiffly disobedient hooks that grasped, released, grasped, released, with greater and greater reluctance.

There was some sort of commotion by the building. Someone called out. A Guardian? At that moment he couldn't have defined a Guardian, and wouldn't have cared. The universe was one hand after another.

It came! He had watched for it each second, and when it came it took him totally by surprise. There was the faintest of tugs at his belt as the free end of the line drew tight, and then, far behind him, the thread whipped away from the tree he had left.

He dropped like a nighthawk.

The ground struck his knee a single, stunning blow and then he was hurtling upward toward the eaves of the Hall. He reached the top of his swing and all the strain was suddenly gone from his arms. For a single, terrifying split-second he was afraid his cramped hands would not let go. Then he was free of the line. He concentrated his whole being into keeping his balance, flexing his knees.

The dark roof came up and took him. He gathered the shock in his thigh-muscles, turned one shoulder down and rolled.

Then for a long, luxurious minute he lay still and rested.

After Bronze shoved the boulder over the edge and roared his terrible challenge into the night, he scuttled like a frightened rabbit through the dark tunnel of a trail that angled down the slope. "Crazy, crazy," he muttered. It couldn't work, that crazy plan of Gesell's. It was marvelous, heroic, brilliant, but—crazy. And he, Bronze, was crazy too, to think of helping. He'd go home. He'd had enough—enough to tell all Prellton about for the rest of his life.

But in spite of his thoughts, his legs carried him cautiously down the slope to the deadly courtyard of Gesell Hall.

"Line," said a low voice.

It was the cowled figure of a Guardian, waiting quietly in the moonlight to unleash hot green death.

"Now I'm going home," thought Bronze, quite coldly and rationally.

He stayed where he was.

Then he saw the other Guardian, moving as if on a track— slowly, steadily, with no hint of a leg-motion—just an inhuman glide. Snails move like that. Centipedes. The stories of monsters from the other side of the Gateway suddenly flooded into his mind.

Bronze saw something else. If the second Guardian moved farther out, away from the Hall, he, Bronze, would be in a straight line between the two of them—

There was an abrupt, intense feeling in his stomach, as if his dinner rabbit had come to life again and had hopped. He rose to his feet. His mouth was dry.

The second Guardian was now out of sight, still moving toward that point which would bracket Bronze in verdant flame.

"Line," said the second voice, and then came the first of the two greatest shocks of Bronze's life.

With a glare of bright white light, a face appeared in midair—twenty feet off the ground—in front of the blank wall of the building.

"Guardian!" sang a deep, organlike voice.

The face was Garth Gesell's.

"Gesell!" gasped a Guardian. Sobbing, he ran toward the light. The other followed slowly. Bronze could begin to see, in the nimbus of light from the radiant face, Gesell's whole body. It hung in the air, perhaps a third of the way down the wall, with one arm thrust forward. The other hand seemed to be behind his back.

"Stop!" intoned the voice. "Remove your habits, Guardians, for I have returned!"

The Guardian from the left faltered, stopped. He stripped off his robe and cast it aside. The other followed suit. The two naked figures moved toward the building, like sleepwalkers. And as they did so, the shining face slid slowly and majestically to the ground. The Guardians fell to their knees and bowed to the earth at his feet. The light disappeared.

"Bronze?" Garth spoke quietly, but the syllable snapped Bronze out of his awed revery. He leapt to his feet and sprinted across the wide court, to receive his second mighty shock.

Garth stood erect against the wall, and Bronze realized the stiffness of utter exhaustion in his stance. "Watch 'em," Garth whispered, and turned his flashlight on the two reverent figures.

One of them was a girl.

The long-tethered wild horses reared up in Bronze's brain. There was an explosion of desire that jolted him to the marrow. He bent quickly and took her arm. "Stand up, you."

She did.

She looked at him from wide, untroubled eyes. She made no attempt to cover herself or to cower. She met his gaze, and simply waited.

There were two kinds of women on earth—the Escaped, and the Returned. The Escaped had been passed over by the hunting Ffanx—by chance, by luck, by sheer animal cunning on the part of the women or the men who hid them. They had been fair game for the Ffanx while the Ffanx ruled Earth, and they were fair game for any of the hundred-odd men who were left to compete for each of them.

And of the earth's few women, perhaps one in a thousand was Returned. Almost invariably the Ffanx had slaughtered the women. But once in a long, long while they let the woman go. Why, no human ever understood. Perhaps it was capriciousness, perhaps it was done for experimentation. But in the rough ethic of a heterogeneous, dark-age society—all that was left of Earth culture after the Ffanx had conquered and then were destroyed in their turn—these women were sacrosanct. They had paid. Their very existence on the planet was a narrative and a dirge; they were the walking sorrow of earth. And they were not to be touched. It was all that could be done for their loss and their loneliness. They knew it, and they walked without fear.

The wild horses within Bronze settled. They gentled, quieted, as if some firm, known hand had touched their flaring nostrils.

"Sister," he said, "I'm sorry."

She barely inclined her head. She turned then to Garth

and said in a low voice, "What can we do for the master?"

Garth sighed. "I have come a long way. My friend and I need rest. Guard as you always have, and in the morning there will be a new day, and nothing will ever be the same again for any of us."

The girl touched the shoulder of the other Guardian. "Come."

He rose. He was a slender, dark-browed youth with the wild frightened eyes of a chipmunk. He had white flesh and stick-like arms, and a very great dignity. "Master," he said to Garth. In his tone was subservience, but an infinitely proud sense of service rather than a humble one. He and the girl went into the building.

"Sexless," said Bronze. It was an identification only, there was no scorn.

Garth said, "I'm tired."

"You sleep. I'll watch," said Bronze.

"You can sleep too," said Garth. "We're in, Bronze. Really in."

"Bronze . . ."

The big man was on his feet, weapons in hand, before Gesell's voice had ceased. He cast about the room, saw no immediate menace, and crossed to the bed. "You all right?"

Garth stretched luxuriously. "Never better, though I feel as if my shoulder-joints needed oiling . . . what's for breakfast?"

Bronze went to the door and flung it open, filling his mighty lungs to shout. He didn't. The girl was standing there, waiting.

Garth saw her. "Come in—Good Lord, girl, you must be freezing!"

"I haven't had your permission . . ." she said gravely.

"Go dress. And tell the other Guardian to put on some clothes. What's your name?"

"Viki."

"What's his name—that other Guardian?"

"Daw, Master."

"Good. My name's not Master. It's Garth, or Gesell, whichever suits you. This is Bronze. Is there anything to eat?"

"Yes, Garth Gesell."

Garth pursed his lips. Her intonation of his name was infinitely more adoring, even, than her "Master." He said, "We'll be out in a minute. I want you to eat with us, do you understand? You and the other, both."

"A great honor, Garth Gesell." She smiled, and it did wonders for the fine-drawn austerity of her face.

She waited a moment, and when Garth apparently had nothing more to say, she left. She backed to the door.

Breakfast was an acutely uncomfortable affair. They ate at a small square table in the hall under the portrait of the first Gesell. It might have been a picture of Garth five or ten years older. They had always looked alike.

Viki, now dressed in the conventional short flowing tunic fastened only by a wide belt, sat demure and quiet, speaking only when spoken to, and screening her constant gaze at Garth with her long lashes. Daw stared straight ahead out of round, permanently astonished eyes, and tried hard, apparently, to avoid looking directly at Gesell. Bronze grinned broadly at Garth's discomfiture and ignored the prim looks of the two Guardians.

Garth waited until the meal was finished, and then put his palms down on the table. "We have work to do."

They turned to him so raptly and obediently that for a moment he lost his train of thought. Bronze looked as if he was about to laugh. Garth shot him a venomous look and said to the Guardians, "But I want you to talk first. I've been away a long time. I want the history of this place as you know it, especially where it concerns the Gateway."

Viki and Daw looked at one another. Garth said, "Come on, come on—"

Daw composed himself, folded his hands on the edge of the table, and cast his eyes down. "In the year of the Ffanx," he intoned, "on the meadows of Hack and Sack, there appeared a blue light shaped like a great arched doorway, filled with a flickering mist."

"We trust in Gesell," muttered Viki.

"And there came from this archway a creature as long as a hand and as heavy as four times its mass in lead castings. It sniffed at the air, and it took up some soil, and it lifted a box which it held to its head, and it smelled out our women. It called, then; and out of the archway came more of its kind in the hundreds of thousands, wearing strange trappings and bringing machines to work evil. And these were the Ffanx."

"We trust in Gesell," murmured the girl.

Garth opened his mouth to speak, and closed it abruptly. He had a quick ear, and he had rapidly caught the cadences of Daw's voice. No one speaks like that naturally. This wasn't a report, it was a singsong ritual.

"At first the world wondered, at first the world laughed at

he Ffanx. For the Ffanx were so tiny, and their ships were like toys, and they spread over Earth without harming a soul, and submitted to capture and acted like comical dolls. They covered the planet and when they were ready—they struck."

He put his head down on his folded hands as he spoke the last two words. Viki droned, "We trust in Gesell."

Daw straightened up and now his voice deepened. His eyes were wide, and fixed on nothing in the room. As he spoke, Garth found himself fascinated by the almost imperceptible motion of Bronze's shaggy head as it nodded in time to the dactylic beat of Daw's speech.

"They struck at our women. They found them in homes and in caves and in churches: killed them by millions. Their weapons were hammers of force from the sky, inaudible sounds that drove strong men to kill their own daughters and slaughter themselves. And then the foul Ffanx would sweep in their bodies.

"And sometimes they herded them, flashing about in their sleek little airships, smashing the men and propelling the foot-weary women along to great pens in the open. They walled them about with their fences of force and destroyed all attacks from outside, and then at their leisure they killed all our females, this one today and then that one, and two or two thousand tomorrow. And Earth saw its blackest, its sorriest day . . .

"Earth was united in madness."

"We trust in Gesell."

"Gesell was a giant who lived on a hill, a worker of wonders who turned from his works to the solving of problems for Earth. Of all men on Earth, he alone learned the nature of Ffanx and the land whence they came and the spell he could cast to destroy them. It was he who devised a retreat for the women that not even Ffanx could detect. He set up a Gateway and passed women through it—women with beauty and women with mind, and any and all of the women with child who could come to the Gateway.

"And the Earth had turned savage, and men lost their reason and stormed up the hill of Gesell, and they tried to pass into the gateway and get to the women. With some it was hunger, with some it was cowardice. So Gesell, all unwilling, constructed defenses, appointed the Guardians, gave instructions to kill all who came in attack, be they human or Ffanx."

"We trust in Gesell."

"And this is the Word of Gesell:

" 'Guard the Gateway with your lives. Make no attempt to open it, or the Ffanx will find it and take the treasure it hides. When the time is right, the women will open the Gateway themselves—or I or another Gesell will open it from this side. But guard it well.'

"That is the Word of Gesell, and the end of his Word; and he alone knows if there was to be more; for that was the end of Gesell. The Ffanx came and killed him, but dying, he cast a great spell and they died. They died on two worlds and the menace is done with. And Earth is in darkness and waits for Gesell to return, and the Gateway to open. And meanwhile the Word of Gesell is the hope of the world:

"Guard the Gateway."

Daw's voice died away. Bronze sat as if mesmerized. Viki's lips moved silently in the response.

Garth slapped his hand down suddenly, shockingly. "This is going to hurt," he gritted. "Daw, where did that—that recitation come from? Where did it start?"

"It's the Word of Gesell," said Daw, wonderingly. "Everybody—"

"We repeat it morning and night," Viki interposed, "to strengthen us in our duty."

"But whose phrases are they? Who made it up?"

"Garth Gesell, *you* must know . . . or perhaps you are testing us."

"Will you answer the question?"

"I learned it from Daw," said Viki.

"I learned it from Soames, who had it from Elbert and Vesta, who were taught by Gesell himself."

Garth closed his eyes. "Elbert . . . Holy smoke! He was the . . ." He stopped himself in time. He remembered Elbert —a dreamy scholar with whom his father used to have long and delightful philosophical discussions, and who, at other times, pushed a broom around the laboratories. Garth began to see the growth of this myth, born in the poetic mind of a misfit.

He looked into their rapt faces. "I'm going to tell you the same story that you told me," he said flatly, "but without the mumbo-jumbo.

"Gesell was my father. He was a great man and a good one. He was *not* nine feet tall, Bronze. And—" he turned to the Guardians—"he was not a 'worker' of spells.

"Now to your legend. 'The meadows of Hack and Sack' are swampland just south of what used to be, before the Ffanx came, the greatest city on Earth. The real name is Hackensack. The blue arch wasn't magic, it was science—it was the same thing as the Gateway itself, though of a slightly different kind.

"The Ffanx were small and heavy because they came from an area where molecular structure is far more compressed than it is here. And they struck at our women for a good reason. It wasn't viciousness and it wasn't for sport. It was, to them, a vital necessity. And that necessity made it useless to think of driving them off, defeating them. They had to be *destroyed*, not defeated. I won't go into the deeper details of inter-dimensional chemistry. But I want you to know exactly what the Ffanx were after—you'll understand them a lot better.

"There is no great difference, physically, between men and women. I mean, bone structure, metabolism, heart and lung and muscular function are different in quality but not in kind. But there is one thing that women produce that men do not. It's a complex protein substance called extradiol. One of its parts is called extradiol *beta-prime*, and is the only way in which human extradiol differs from that of other female animals. With it, they're women. Without it, they're nothing . . . cold, sexless . . . ruined.

"So it was this substance that the Ffanx were after. You've heard the tales of what they wanted. Women. But they didn't want them as women. They were after *extradiol* for the best reason on Earth or off it: ·

"It made them immortal!"

Bronze's jaw dropped. Viki continued to gaze raptly at Garth. Daw's heavy brows were drawn together in an expression that looked more like fear and worry than perplexity.

"Think about that for a minute. Think of what would happen if we of Earth found a species of animal which carried a substance which would do that for us . . . we'd hunt it ruthlessly and mercilessly."

"Wait a minute," Bronze said. "You mean that these Ffanx couldn't die from a spear-wound?"

"Lord, no—they weren't immortal in that sense. Just from old age which, in any species, is a progressive condition caused by dysfunction of various parts—particularly connective tissue. A complicated extract containing human extradiol *beta* would restore the connective tissues of the Ffanx and keep them healthy for thirty of our years or more. Then another shot would keep 'em that way, and so on."

"Just where is the Ffanx world?" asked Daw, and then

colored violently as if embarrassed by the sound of his own voice.

"That's a little difficult to explain," said Garth carefully. "Look, suppose that door—" he pointed to an interior doorway—"opened into more than one room. You can almost imagine it; say you'd have to go through the door from an acute angle to get into the first room, go straight through to get into a second. You might call the second world Parallel X.

"The Gateway and the blue arch at Hackensack were doorways between worlds—between universes. These universes exist at the same time in the same space—but at different vibratory rates . . . I don't expect you to understand it, no one really does. The theory's an old one. No one gave it much consideration until the Ffanx got here."

Bronze asked, "If it's a doorway, like you say, why didn't the Ffanx find the way in to the world where the women went?"

Garth smiled. "Remember the doorway there? Suppose you were quite familiar with the way that door opened to one of two rooms. Then supposing I came along and pointed out that instead of going straight in or turning left, you could go *up* and find yourself in still a third room. It's like that. The Ffanx just never thought of going into their inter-dimensional arch in the particular direction that would wind them up in the Gateway world.

"There was always the possibility that the Ffanx *might* think of it, though, and you can bet that the women were warned and were ready to fight. But to get back to the story—I have to tell it all to you so you can understand what we're going to do next; and I will have you understand it, because I don't want help from people who just take orders, I want help from people who think.

"All right, let's go on. I'm trying to give you an idea of what my father was—a man who worked and worried and made mistakes and was happy and frightened and brave and all the other things you are.

"He was a scientist, a specialist in molecular structure. In the early days of the invasion he got hold of a couple of Ffanx. You'll remember that they weren't attacking then. My Dad was the only man who was ever able to communicate with them, and he did it without their realizing what he was doing. A specialist in condensed matter can produce a lot of weird effects. One of the things he found out was that thought itself is a vibration very similar to the brainwaves of a Ffanx-type mind; that is, the currents that produced thought in their brains could be changed directly into waves his instruments could detect and translate. He got no details, but he did get some broad concepts. One of them was that the blue arch was the only exit that they had ever made from their world; they had never traveled to other planets in their universe. Another was the nature of their quest on Earth. When he found that out, he killed his specimens, but by then it was too late.

"He took those little bodies apart literally atom by atom. And he found out how to destroy them. It was simple in itself, but hard to get to, an isotope of nitrogen which, if released in their world, would set up a chain reaction in their atmosphere. Due to the differences between the molecules of the two universes—they have a table of elements just like ours, but denser—their atmospheric hydrogen could be transmuted to free hydrogen and arsenic tri-hydride, with a by-product of nitrogen ions that would kick off the reaction again and again ... I see I'm talking gobbledegook. Sorry.

"Suffice it to say that my father knew what would destroy the Ffanx, but he had to make it himself. By that time the Ffanx had destroyed communications and the world was in chaos. It took time, as he knew it would. So he built the Gateway.

"He got the idea from the Ffanx' own blue arch, which he had seen from a distance. He took careful reading on that strange blue light and guessed what it was. He came back here and proved what it was. And in trying to build another like it—I think he planned to invade them where they didn't expect it—he stumbled on the Gateway.

"It gave a weird red-orange light instead of a blue one, and the atmosphere on the other side was breathable, which the Ffanx world's was not—they had to wear helmets and carry an air-supply while they were on Earth. He went through and looked the place over. There was timber and water and, as far as he could find out, no civilization or dangerous animals—just insects and some little rabbit-like creatures so tame they could be caught by hand. And he got the idea of using it as a sanctuary for the world's women while he worked on the weapon that would destroy the Ffanx.

"You know the rest of that story—how the women came, all he could send word to—and then how he had to build defenses against the panic-struck, woman-hungry mobs that stormed this place.

"I was just a boy of eight when Dad finished the weapon. It was an innocent-looking eight-inch capsule filled with compressed gas. He planned to go up to Hackensack, traveling at night and hiding in the daytime, and set up a projector to peg it into the blue arch.

"The day after he showed it to me the Ffanx came . . . I'm convinced they didn't know how near they were to the thing that would wipe them out. I'll never know why they came just then . . . maybe there was a party of women on the way up the canyon. Anyway, a flight of their little ships appeared, and they let go one of their force-beams on the lab-building—I guess because it was the nearest to the canyon trail—and stove the roof in. Dad was crushed and the building burned."

Garth took a deep breath. His eyes burned. "I spoke to him while he died. Then I left, with the capsule."

"So it was you who put the poison through the blue arch," said Bronze. "I'd always heard it was Gesell."

"It was Gesell," said Viki devoutly.

"I did, yes. Anyway, when that capsule burst in their world, they had a fine arseniated atmosphere. The hydrogen they breathed was arsenic tri-hydride within minutes after it got to their bloodstreams. I don't know how long it took to kill off every last one of them on their planet, but it couldn't have been long. And it got all the Ffanx here, too. They all had to go back to renew their air supplies. I don't think we'll ever hear of a living Ffanx again."

"And where have you been all these years?"

"Growing up. Studying. Dad's orders. He was the most foresighted man who ever lived. He couldn't be sure of just what would happen in the near future, but he knew what the possibilities were, and acted on all of them. One of the things he did was to prepare a hypnopede—it's a gadget that teaches you while you sleep—no bigger than your two fists. It was designed for me, in case anything happened, and it covered the basic principles of the Gateway, and a long list of reference books. I lived with that thing, month after month, and when I was old enough to move around safely under my own power I began to travel. I went to city after city and pawed through the ruins of their libraries and boned up on all of it—atomic theory, strength of materials, higher math, electronics—until I could begin to get experimental results."

He looked around the table. "Are you people ready to give me a hand with the Gateway?"

"We took a vow——" said Viki. Garth interrupted her. "Let's have none of that!"

Viki continued with perfect composure. "We took a vow to serve Gesell through life and past death, and I see no reason to change it. Do you, Daw?"

"I agree." Daw's face was strained. Garth thought for a second that Daw was going to argue the point. But perhaps he was wrong . . .

"Good," said Garth. "Now—when the Ffanx destroyed the laboratory, they smashed the Gateway generators, as you know. I think I can restore them. With your help I know I can."

"Hey wait," said Bronze. "What about that prediction that the women would open it from the other side?"

"They're supposed to have the facilities," said Garth. "There's just one piece of evidence we have that proves we've got to do it—they haven't opened the Gateway."

"Why not, d'you suppose?"

Garth shrugged. "Afraid to, maybe. Maybe something's happened to them. Who knows? Let's find out."

Viki spoke up, timidly. "Garth Gesell—it's been years since they went through. Will they be . . . I mean, do you suppose there are . . ." She floundered to a halt.

"Even women in their late thirties and forties can do some good to the world now," Garth answered. "And don't forget—many of them were with child. There'll be new blood for Earth. However, one of the most important considerations is the women themselves. Among them were some of the best brains on Earth. Architects and doctors, and even a machine-tool designer. But the biggest treasure of all is Glory Rehman. She was my Dad's friendly enemy—almost as good as he was in his specialty, and a lot better in several more. If she's still alive, she'll do more to get the world back on its feet than any thousand people alive today. You'll see . . . you'll see. Come on, let's get to work!"

The days that followed were a haze of activity. Garth traced the old power-supply, and to his delight found it in prime condition. It had been used for little but the Guardian's flame, all other equipment having been pretty well smashed or gone into disuse. The super-batteries which fed it were neo-tourmaline, a complex crystal that had the power of storing enormous quantities in its facets. Garth's first task was to restore the great sundishes which charged the crystals.

His father had designed them to replace the broadcast power that he had used before he developed the condensed-matter crystal.

The Guardians—Garth had abandoned that term, but Bronze still insisted on using it—worked like beavers—Viki worshipfully and silently, Daw in a feverish way which puzzled Garth and angered Bronze. Bronze himself had to be watched to keep him from bossing the others. Garth kept him under control by doubting aloud whether he could do this or that, or by wondering if he was strong enough to move this over to there. "You think I can't," Bronze would mutter, and attack the task as if it were a deadly enemy.

Twice Garth called them all into the new laboratory and announced that the Gateway was ready. The first time nothing happened when he threw the switch, and it took him eight days to trace out the circuits and to test the vibratory controls. The second time a sheet of cool orange flame leaped into being, quivered and flickered for a moment, and then collapsed.

At each of these occasions Bronze berated Garth for letting the Guardians see it. "Here you got them thinking you're a superman," he said disgustedly, "and then you let them watch you pull a blooper."

Garth was alone in the makeshift laboratory when he succeeded. He had bent to replace a crystal which was a few thousandths of a cycle out of phase, and he turned back to the Gateway apparatus—and there it was.

Quietly, noiselessly, it hung there, so beautiful it made him gasp, so welcome he could hardly believe his eyes. It was red-orange at the bottom, shading to gold at the top.

He spun to the switch. It was still open. Then he realized that his synchronization of the quartz frequency-crystals and the tourmaline power-crystals was so perfect that the Gateway had come of its own accord. He had known that the phenomenon was self sustaining, he hadn't known that it was self-starting.

He closed the switch as a safety-measure, and stood looking at the Gateway. "Got it," he muttered. And he could all but feel his father's presence with him, dark eyes glowing, his hand ready with the reward the boy used to prize so highly—the warm clasp of a shoulder.

Garth glanced at the door, thinking of Bronze and the others. Then he shrugged. "Let 'em sleep. They'll need it."

He stepped through the Gateway.

In her small cell Viki slept lightly. She was dreaming about Gesell, as she often did. Her early training with old Soames had been partly hypnopedic, and like most sleep-training, it tended to be restimulated by sleep itself. Part of it pictorialized itself in a dream of the main foyer in Gesell Hall, where the great portrait of Gesell hung. She seemed to be watching the picture, which refused to be a picture of the elder Gesell, but of Garth. And as she watched, the long, white browed face began to turn pale. The face was composed, but the eyes conveyed a worriment that grew into terror and then into agony. As she stared at it, frozen, the dream picture suddenly ripped down the middle with a sound she was never to forget as long as she lived.

She bounded out of bed and stood gasping in the middle of the floor. Her sense of presence returned to her. She glanced around her and then bolted for the door.

In a silent panic she raced for the laboratory, threw the door open.

Between the tall grid-electrodes over which Garth had slaved for so many weeks there was a sheet of flame. Viki stared at it, awed, and then realized what was so very strange about it; it radiated no heat. She approached it cautiously.

On the floor by the lower frame of the apparatus lay a human hand.

She knew that hand. Heaven knows she had spent enough mealtimes watching its deft movement from under her lowered lashes. She had seen it probing the complexities of the apparatus often enough, and had marveled at its skilled strength.

"Garth Gesell . . ." she moaned.

She stooped over the hand and only then did she realize that it was thrust through the flame as if through a curtain.

She seized it and pulled. She saw the forearm, the elbow . . . "Bronze!" she screamed. She set her small bare feet against the lower frame and lifted and pulled.

Garth Gesell's body slid out. It was flecked with blood. Blood flowed slowly from his nostrils and ears. His lifeless face held just the expression of terror and agony she had seen in her dream. His flesh was mottled and his lips were blue.

She screamed again, a wordless cry of fury at the fates rather than one of fear. She flipped the body over on its face, turned the head to one side, put her fingers in the unresisting mouth and drew the tongue forward. Then she knelt with her left knee between his thighs and began to apply artificial respiration. "Bronze!" She called again and again, with each measured pressure of her sure hands.

Bronze appeared at the door, looking like a war-horse, his nostrils dilated, his muscular chest gleaming with sweat. "What is—what are you doing to him?" He strode forward, his big hand out to pluck her away from Gesell.

She put her head back and said "Stop." It was said quietly but with such intensity that he halted as if he had run onto a wagon-tongue in the dark. Daw came in, rubbing his eyes.

She ignored the men. She lay down on the floor beside Garth and put her face next to his.

"Viki!" said Daw in horror. "Your vows . . ."

"Shut up," she hissed, and put her mouth against Garth's. Bronze said "What the hell's she . . ."

"Leave her," said Daw in a new voice.

Bronze's startled expression matched Daw's natural one. Bronze followed his gaze. Exactly in synchronization, Viki's cheeks and Garth's expanded and relaxed. In the sudden silence, they could hear the breath whistle in Viki's arched nostrils.

"Gesell . . ." whispered Viki hoarsely. She put her mouth against Garth's again.

Suddenly his head jerked back. Feebly, he coughed.

"She did it," muttered Bronze. "Viki—you did it."

Viki rolled like a cat and bounded to her feet. She dipped her hand in a waterbucket and sloshed the freezing mass into the middle of Garth's back. He gasped, a great gulping inhalation, and began to cough again. "Get alcohol," said Viki tightly.

They rolled Garth over and Daw lifted his head. They forced a few drops of ethyl alcohol into Garth's mouth. He shuddered.

"Somebody kissed me," he said. He lay back, breathing deeply. "The . . . Gateway . . . women are dead. It's no use."

"What was it?" asked Daw. "Was the air poisonous?"

"No . . . it was all right—what there was of it. There just wasn't enough. I don't know what caused it, but something has used up most of the air in that world. I passed out before I'd gone any real distance. And the women . . ."

"Didn't you see any signs of them?"

"Not a thing. The world seemed empty. Parallel X . . ."

There was a silence. Then Garth asked, "Well—where do we go from here?"

Daw suddenly leaped to his feet. "Gesell!" he cried. "Great Gesell, forgive me!"

Garth looked up at him curiously. "Daw I've told you a thousand times not to call me—"

"You!" spat Daw. "You—imposter! You apostate! You're the devil! You came here in the guise of the great Gesell in order to invade the sanctuary of Gesell's women. No Gesell would tire, no Gesell would fail. No Gesell would respond to the clutches of a female."

Bronze was on his feet. "Now, listen, you—"

Daw threw out his skinny arms dramatically. "Go on— kill me; I deserve a hundred deaths for my failure as a Guardian. But I die in defense of Gesell and his works. It's the least I can do." He suddenly flew at Bronze. "Kill me now— kill me!"

Bronze put out one mighty arm and caught the front of Daw's tunic. Daw flailed away helplessly. His arms were far shorter than Bronze's, and all he could do was to rain blows on the iron biceps and kick feebly at the man's boots.

"What shall I do?" said the amazed Bronze. "Shall I squash him?"

"Don't harm him," said Garth. "But I guess you better put him to sleep."

Bronze brought his free hand up and over and put a hammerlike blow on the very top of Daw's head. The little Guardian went limp. Bronze draped him across the crook of his elbow like a spare blanket.

"What about you?" he said to the girl.

Viki stared up at him out of wide eyes and turned to Garth. "I serve Gesell."

Garth said tiredly. "There seem to be three Gesells around here. My Dad, who's dead. Me. And some sort of King Arthur-type myth. Which one are you serving?"

"Only you," she breathed. She rose gracefully, cast a look of utmost scorn at the feebly twitching Daw, excused herself and left the room.

"Let her go," said Garth to Bronze.

"She's liable to blow up the joint," protested Bronze.

"I think not."

"You can be wrong, Garth Gesell."

Garth grinned wryly. "You know that, and still you stick around. I wish these dedicated characters felt the same way. I just can't live up to what they want me to be."

"Maybe you can't," growled Bronze. "But you should. I

told you and told you you should." He hefted Daw. "What'll we do with this?"

"Try to talk some sense into him."

"Let me twist his head off first. Then you can put the sense in with a trowel."

Garth chuckled. "That won't be necessary. I know what's wrong with him. Bronze, many people who take readily to dedicated service do it only because it's a substitute for ordinary living, which they don't want to face. That isn't by any means true of all of 'em, but it is of our boy here. Life these days isn't easy, I don't have to tell you that. As a Guardian, Daw had an even, dependable existence where he knew what he had to do and knew exactly how to do it. He saw no reason why that should ever change. And then I came along and reduced him to the level of a guy who is changing his environment a lot now so that it can be changed still more later, and he didn't like it."

"That sounds good. Now can you pound that all into his head with one wallop? Or shall I stand guard over him for a year or so while you lead him by the hand out of a swamp he made himself to wallow in?"

"Easy, easy," said Garth ruefully.

"Dammit, you need it," growled Bronze. "Something's wrong with the Gateway world. Something was wrong with your idea of walking into Gesell Hall that day I met you, but that didn't stop you." Bronze wet his lips. "I guess I'm a little like that Daw, after all. You got to be what I think you should be before I'll play along with you."

They found Viki in the laboratory, staring at the Gateway, which flamed and flickered coldly in its frames. Garth and Bronze ranged up beside her.

"If we could only move around in there," said Garth. "If we could only know what happened to the air-pressure."

"The Ffanx did it," said Viki.

"Let him do the thinking, sister," said Bronze with the odd combination of bluntness and courtesy he affected with her.

"There are no more Ffanx, Viki," said Garth. "If I'm sure of anything, I am sure of that."

"I know that," said Viki. "I mean that the Ffanx moved from dense air into rarefied air—you said so."

Garth struck himself a resounding wallop on the forehead. "Bronze," he said in an awed tone of voice, "she has the brains."

"Huh?"

"Air helmets! Here I was so defeated that I couldn't see the one thing that was staring me in the face. Come on. The machine shop!"

The helmets they turned out in the next few days were makeshift but serviceable. Using the domed tops of aluminum pressure tanks and a series of welded bands, and a tightly-gasketed piece of plexiglas, they had the basic design. Soft, thick edging of foam rubber sealed the shoulder, chest and back. The air supply was liquid air passed through a tiny but highly efficient chemical heater. "We want no oxygen drunks on this trip," Garth explained.

They locked Daw up in the north storeroom. Garth tried to talk to him but found him completely intractable. He was like a man in a trance. He would speak only to the original Gesell, using his name to call down maledictions on the heads of the imposters.

"What shall we take with us?"

They stood before the Gateway—Bronze impatient and excited, Garth thoughtful, Viki her reserved, willing self. Green floodlights and a smoke generator had been strategically placed on the defense line in the canyon, keyed to the detectors so that any intruder would be badly frightened if he came onto the Court. It was defense enough for the short time they planned to be away.

"My spears," said Bronze.

"No," Garth said. "Take this instead." He tossed over his old blaster. "It's more compact. I mean no insult to that throwing arm of yours, little man, but the blaster has a little more range."

"Thanks." Bronze turned it over admiringly. "Did I ever tell you that if you hadn't been carrying this when I first met you I'd have knocked you off? I never met a man with one before."

Garth laughed. "I hadn't had charges for it for more than four years. It was good protective coloration. But there are plenty of charges now. Viki—"

"I have my dagger. And an extra air tank."

"Good. I'll take two extra tanks. That ought to hold us.

"Now here's the plan. We have no radio. I was able to weld in some thin plates to my helmet—I should be able to hear in there. I don't think you two will be able to unless you touch helmets. I won't be able to hear you but I can hear outside sounds. So once we get in there, we're pretty much on our own. All I can say is—keep together and don't go too far. Mind you, this is just a preliminary recon patrol. Later we can go back in with more and better equipment. Ready?"

Bronze raised a thumb and forefinger in the ancient sign. "Right!" Viki nodded tensely.

Garth wheeled, settled his helmet down on its shoulder-pieces. The others followed suit.

Then Garth plunged through the Gateway.

The three huddled together as they emerged from the Gateway.

They found themselves on a stony plain that stretched out and away as far as the eye could reach. There were the looming shadows of distant, tremendous mountains. The rocks were soft and coarse, and of the same orange-to-gold shading that characterized the Gateway.

Garth glanced around at the Gateway, and understood how in his previous visit he had missed it. It flickered and flamed as dimly as a candle in the sunlight. He touched his two companions and pointed back at it. They nodded, and he knew they understood the need for caution. In that wilderness of boulders it would be easy to lose it completely.

He recalled the first Gateway, his father's, which had debouched on a flat plain, smaller than this. There had been rocks here and there, but nothing like the monstrous, crumbling boulders which surrounded them now. He wondered, as he had many times in the past few days, if the elder Gesell's specifications had been wrong in some subtle way, and if this was, as Bronze had suggested, a different dimensional world from that to which the women had been sent. In the maze of advanced mathematics involved in the construction of a Gateway, any small slip might have far-reaching results.

His thought broke off abruptly. Through the two thin discs welded into the sides of his helmet he could hear a highpitched, shattering roar. He looked up—

It was a helicopter—but such a machine as a mad aeronautical engineer might dream of in a nightmare!

It was huge and it was slow. It was altogether too slow. Its great blades had a radius of nearly two hundred feet. It settled downward much faster than it seemed to, for its size was so deceptive; the vanes rotated no faster than the wings of an ancient Dutch windmill.

It came to rest a hundred yards away. Its size was incredible. As it rested on the ground, the roof of the fuselage was all of eighty feet from the ground. The door opened.

Garth swept the helmets of the other two against his with one motion. They contacted with a deafening clang.

"Hide!" he barked. "In the rocks . . . get out of sight!"

He turned and dove for shelter. Just to his right a huge flat rock, which had apparently once stood on edge, leaned over at about eighty degrees. Under it was just enough space for him to slide into with his helmet protruding.

He looked first for his companions. Bronze was huddled behind a round boulder. Viki was running back toward the Gateway, zigzagging in a panic-struck search for adequate shelter. He saw her trip and fall, and an airtank went bounding away from her shoulder. She rose groggily to her feet and tried to run again.

Garth looked back toward the helicopter. What he saw confirmed the surge of fear he had experienced as its door had opened.

Four women approached with great leaping strides. They were dressed in odds and ends—a ragged halter, a smooth tunic, a slashed skirt. Each was dressed differently and casually. One carried a monstrous knobbed club. All were belted and had long daggers. Around the neck of the leader was a black chain from which swung a mighty jewel, which glowed and sparkled in the universally orange-gold light. The jewel was brilliantly, shockingly green—the characteristic glittering green of neo-tourmaline. But Garth had never seen a crystal of that size. It was gem-cut, and must have been all of forty inches from crown to apex. And the woman carried it comfortably at the end of its ten-foot stick-like mounting, on its chain with links the size of anchor-cable, because she herself was seventy-five feet tall.

Garth was conscious of a pounding in his ears. At first he thought it was the earth-shaking tread of the four giantesses —for the other three were almost as tall as the first. Then he realized that the pounding was caused by the simple fact that in his shock he had forgotten to breathe.

He turned and looked for his companions. Bronze was slack and awed, gaping skyward at the leader's tremendous head. Viki was nowhere to be seen—

And neither was the Gateway. It was gone.

The leader stopped not twenty yards away, and bent, scanning the ground, fingering her jewelled pendant. Her face was distant, composed and cool. She was very beautiful, with long-lashed eyes and high-arched brows and a complexion like unveined marble.

"Bronze!" Garth screamed, for the second woman, a blonde with masses of flowing golden hair, had circled, and was behind Bronze as he stared up at the leader. The blonde raised her club, a thirty-foot mass that must have weighed all of a ton. She spoke—a deep, unintelligible strumming. Bronze, of course, could not hear Garth's cry of warning.

The leader straightened up and glanced at the blonde. She said something equally incomprehensible—the frequency of their voice-tones was down in the subsonic—and the blonde reluctantly put down the club.

And then, to Garth's horror, the leader bent and shot out a mighty hand. Bronze tried to scuttle aside, but the hand closed on him, lifted him high in the air.

Then it was that Garth recognized the giantess. He knew he had seen that cool, beautiful face before—long, long before, when he was a child.

Bronze squirmed and fought that gigantic grip. Garth saw him twist free, ball up and kick with both feet at the huge thumb. He slipped out of the grasp when the hand had carried him forty feet in the air. The giantess fell to one knee and reached out, catching him deftly. She held him up before her great calm face and watched him squirm.

Bronze suddenly struck out with both hands, twisted to one side, and got his hand on the blaster.

"Don't Don't" screamed Garth. He knew what that blaster could do at short range. But his raging was useless, he could not be heard.

The giantess fumbled for a second and then, with her left hand, brought up the pendant by its stick-like handle. She held the jewel close to Bronze as if it were a strange magnifying glass.

Bronze whipped the blaster out and up, and just as it bore on the huge, calm face, the great thumb moved on a stud on the handle of the jewel-mounting.

A blaze of green fire reached out from the jewel and enveloped Bronze's chest, turning to dazzling white where it struck him. The jewel deepened in color and seemed to thicken, to grow more solid.

The magnetic buckles of Bronze's helmet harness suddenly parted, and the internal pressure did the rest. The helmet popped off his head and flew up and around, swinging by the one back strap that was caught between his waist and the imprisoning hand.

Then the blaster spoke.

"Don't!" screamed Garth uselessly. That's Glory Gehman!"

But instead of the shattering roar he expected, his ear-plates detected only a muffled f-f-ft! A weak tongue of fire, perhaps ten or twelve inches long, flickered wanly from the bore of the blaster, and then faded. Bronze writhed once, then went limp.

The great figure that looked like Glory Gehman held Bronze up like a tiny limp doll and called to the other women. They crowded around. The blond reached with long, delicate fingers and lifted up the dangling helmet, pointed at Glory Gehman's ears. Garth noticed for the first time that her ear-pendants were made of Ffanx helmets, or rather a tremendously oversize version of them. The leader shook her head and laughed, and gently forced Bronze's helmet back on his head. Holding her face very close, as if she were threading a needle in bad light, she set the buckle-magnets back in their grooves and gently tested the air-lines. Then the leader walked off toward the helicopter, while the other three resumed their search of the ground.

Garth's eye caught a glint of metal a few yards away—the spare airtank Viki had dropped. But of Viki there was no sign, and gone, too, was the Gateway.

Garth Gesell was alone on this earth, a pygmy hiding under a rock like a beetle, while he was being hunted by colossi obviously bent on destroying his kind.

A great bare foot pressed the earth close to him. He could hear the stones crackle. He crept farther back in the narrow fissure which held him. He knew that the next step the giantess took might be on top of that flat rock, and that would be the end of Gesell on any world save for a revered memory.

And a fat lot of good the reverence would do him as he lay crushed under a rock.

"For Gesell," sang Daw as he hooked the cable around the frame of the Gateway. Then something struck his back and side and sent him sprawling. He kept his hold on the cable as he fell, and part of him was gratified to feel it catch on the frame. He knew it had contacted, and he knew it without looking at the Gateway for the flickering gold light was abruptly gone.

He rolled and came up on one knee.

Lying on the floor, doubled up in pain as she nursed a bleeding foot, was Viki. She squeezed her eyes as tight as they would shut, even through the thick transparent plastic of her helmet Daw could see the silent tears she forced out.

She sat up and looked around her, then sprang to her feet and leaped to the framework. That brought her up against the rear wall of the laboratory. She stood for a moment feeling it with incredulous fingers, then turned and stepped out again.

Apparently it was only then that she saw Daw.

She slid the magnetic buckles apart and wrenched off her helmet. Her hair and eyes were wild.

"Daw. The Gateway!"

"A false Gateway for a false Gesell," intoned Daw.

She looked around at the dead framework again, and then at Daw. "What are you doing here?"

"The hand of Gesell freed me for his good works," said Daw. "I found a weak spot in the ceiling of the storeroom. Now, more than ever, I know the truth and reason behind my act. For you were spared, sister, spared from your own infamies, and saved, as a sworn Guardian, for the true Gesell."

She looked at him, bewildered.

He explained to her, patiently, exultantly. "You were led to return from the company of evil, just as I obeyed Gesell's command to do away with the false Gateway."

"Return? I didn't return!" she said frantically. "I fell. I was running, looking back and up at—at—" She closed her eyes and shuddered. "And then I hurt my foot, and fell . . . Daw, what has happened to the Gateway?"

"Gone," he said, and smiled. "And good riddance. Come, sister. Let us go to the great portrait and receive more messages."

"Daw, we've got to fix it! He's in trouble. They'll kill him, they'll kill him!"

"You confirm it. Death to the imposter! It is Gesell's will!"

Understanding dawned on Viki. "You closed it?"

He bowed his head. "It was the wish of Gesell. I am but a poor instrument . . ."

She was on him like a tiger-cat. "You fool! You crazy, blind fool! Show me what you did. We've got to fix it. We've got to, Daw. Garth Gesell is the true Gesell, don't you understand? And he'll die in there if we don't help him!"

"That Gateway," said Daw in stentorian tones, "is a falsehood, a devil's trick. When Gesell wants it to open he will open it, without wires and crystals and steel. As a Guardian I shall see the end of this contraption, and never again will I be duped." He turned, his eyes blazing, and caught up a sledge hammer. "Never again will there be a Gateway in Gesell Hall until Gesell himself opens it!"

"Daw you're mad! Stop!"

He stalked past her. She took one step after him and stopped. She saw the hooked piece of cable Daw had dropped. She leapt forward, caught up the free end, and as Daw raised the hammer high over his head, his right foot placed itself near the hook.

Viki stepped to one side, to be sure of a good contact, and pulled the cable violently. The hooked end caught Daw's ankle, whipped it out from under him. He staggered, lost control of the hammer. The twelve-pound head fell toward him. He lurched aside and it caught him on the shoulder. He fell heavily, trying to turn. His jaw cracked against the stone floor.

He lay still, uttering a series of tortured sounds as he tried to pull himself together.

Viki stood over him like an avenging angel, waiting.

Daw rolled over, sat up. His hand went quiveringly to his shoulder. He looked up at her out of round, bloodshot eyes.

"Guardian . . ." he said.

"Help me fix the Gateway, Daw," she said.

"You're misled, sister."

"I won't discuss it with you. And don't start that cant about my sacred duty. Get up!"

Daw rose and fixed her with his made eyes. "I am counselled by Gesell," he said painfully, "and now I counsel you."

She closed her eyes in a visible effort at self-control. "Are you going to help me?"

"Why do you pursue this folly? What is the compulsion of this—this Garth?" The last word came out with contempt.

"I love him," she said.

There was a crashing silence. It was the silence of utter shock—the silence of death itself, for indeed nothing moved, not even breath.

Finally Daw's suddenly white lips moved, slackened, moved again. "You love him," he whispered. "You?"

She was just as pale. "We all have our own kind of cowardice," she said. "Bronze once told me what Garth Gesell thought of your madness. He said you were a Guardian because you had retired from a real world. You've gone mad trying to save the old ways for yourself. You can doom the world to the new savagery if by doing it you can return to patrolling the Court and humbling yourself before the portrait."

Daw half raised his arms as if to ward off her hot words. He kept his eyes fixed on her, and when she stopped he said only,

"You're Escaped!"

"Yes!" she cried, "Damn you! You never knew, did you? One of the rules you made up for yourself was that only the poor robbed hulk of a woman, with her womanhood completely gone, could become a Guardian. It's what you chose to believe and what I let you believe. I told you we all have our form of cowardice. Mine was to pretend I was Returned. I stole the privilege of those poor creatures who had been discarded by the Ffanx. I lived with them and learned their ways. They walk in safety all over the world, and I took their coloration. And when the chance came to hide further under the cowl of a Guardian, I took it. I let myself sleep safely here. But I'm awake now . . ." Her lower lip became full, and her eyes grew very bright. ". . . awake and I love him, I love him, I love him . . ."

She lapsed into silence. She heard Daw grind his teeth.

"Slut!" he said hoarsely. "To think that for these years I've been living next to a—a—" In his mounting rage he stopped using words, and instead uttered a series of creaking, dripping animal sounds.

"Now that we know what we are, Guardian," she said coldly, "Let's fix the Gateway."

"I am the Guardian and I am the Gateway, and in me alone is the trust, the duty, the fidelity, the—"

Suddenly he was upon her, raging. Gone was the last vestige of control. Gone was the carefully schooled impersonality of Guardian behavior, gone was the deeply conditioned, pitying reverence for the woman Returned.

His wild leap bowled her off her feet. They rolled over and over on the floor. Daw didn't strike out at her with fists; he clawed. He pulled her hair and her clothes. He raked his fingernails down her body, twisted her, grasped and clutched and pawed.

At first she tried to get away, to protect herself. She writhed and scrambled and fell and pushed at him. Suddenly he was kneeling by her, both hands full of her hair, both arms stiff, pinning her head down to the floor. The pain of her scalp turned to terror—a roweling primitive terror that was like nothing she had ever known in intensity. And in the briefest moments it was surpassed by another, new emotion.

She had been afraid before, in her life, but this was something different.

For as he bent over her, brought his face close to her, she looked up into his eyes. They were round, staring, veined and toned with red. His jaws were open, and his bitten, bloody tongue flashed insanely in and out. Blood and froth splashed on her face, and at its touch, this transcending new emotion overtook her like a great flood-tide.

It was more than horror. It was disgust and revulsion raised to a peak almost impossible to contain. In one great surge she rose. She felt her hair tear away with a kind of savage joy. How she found the holds she never was to know, but one slim hand fastened into the side of Daw's neck and the other on his thigh. She sprang straight up under him with her feet solidly planted and every dyne of energy in her healthy legs, back and shoulders behind the movement. Daw's body went straight up.

When the weight came off her hands he was nearly at arm's length over her head. She dug in her nails and kept her grip, and as he began to fall she pulled hard with her left hand, which was on his neck. Head down he hurtled, with all her convulsive strength speeding him on his way. He struck . . .

For a long time she stood like a cast-iron statue, her unseeing eyes on the thing which lay there, its misshapen head all but concealed, twisted grotesquely under the scrawny body. Then she became dimly conscious of an ache that became a pain that became a roaring agony—the knotting muscles in her calves, cramping with the onset of nervous shock. She tottered backwards, brought up against the wall.

She crouched there, breathing in great open-throated gasps. Suddenly she began to cry—high, squeaky crying that tore her throat and burned her eyes. She cried for a long time.

But the next day, and the next and the next, found her working.

Garth lay under the rock, his heart beating suffocatingly, but his eyes studying the amazing spread of calloused flesh that was the giant foot. Another came down beside it, and the first one lifted and kicked over a massive boulder nearby. Garth felt his sheltering rock vibrate alarmingly. He bunched his shoulders and waited.

At last the feet moved away. He edged out and lay prone, hardly daring to lift his head. The three women were working away from him, scanning the ground carefully. He got on all fours and scuttled backward into the shadow of a projecting rock, pulled himself to his feet and looked around.

The Gateway was gone. Viki was gone—probably through the Gateway, he surmised. Bronze was gone—captured certainly, dead probably. He wondered what that green fire had been. It looked like neo-tourmaline, but the rays had not burned Bronze's body, at least not as far as he had been able to see. It was a little like the damper crystals that his father had developed, to capture and store energy.

But a crystal as big as that, with the pulling power it must have, couldn't be turned on a human being without snuffing out the man's tiny store of electro-chemical.

"Bronze . . ." he said aloud.

Big, bluff, faithful Bronze, with his quick temper and his hammer-thinking. Garth got a flash of memory—Bronze's face when Garth had pulled him up short, pointing out some end result of Bronze's impulsiveness. He used to get a puzzled, slightly hurt expression on his broad face, but he always began nodding his head in agreement before he had figured out if Garth was right or not.

Garth's eyes felt hot. Then, with a profound effort of will, he shut his mind to his regrets and concentrated on his surroundings.

Moving carefully, he worked his way over to the spare tank that Viki had dropped. He worried it in between the two tanks he already carried. He'd live a little longer with it. "Though what for," he muttered, "I wouldn't know." He gave a last, despairing glance to the site of the Gateway and began to move toward the distant helicopter.

A hundred feet away he found a leaf—a tremendous thing, eleven feet long and nearly five feet broad at its widest. He picked it up gratefully. It was very light and spongy. He pulled the stem over his shoulder and walked through the rocks, dragging it. The leaf was almost exactly the color of the soil, and ideal camouflage. All he need do would be to drop it flat and pull it over himself.

He was two-thirds of the way to the plane when a thudding from the earth warned him. He looked back and saw the three women coming rapidly. They seemed to be sauntering, but their stride was twenty to twenty-five feet, and they covered ground at a frightening pace. He dropped and covered himself. The steps came nearer and nearer, until he wondered how the earth itself stood up under that monstrous tread. Then they were past. He got up. They walked with their heads up, talking their booming syllables. They were obviously searching no longer.

He began to run. He had no choice except to stay with these creatures. What he would do, where he would go if they took off, he simply did not know.

They climbed into the cabin, one by one. He could see the landing gear—tremendous wheels as tall as a two-story house —spread as they took the weight of the giants.

There was a belly-thumping cough and the incredible rotor-blades began to turn.

Garth flung down his leaf and ran straight toward the ship, trusting to luck that he wouldn't be seen. When he was under the slow-whirling-tips of the rotor he still had what seemed an impossible distance to run. He found some more energy somewhere and applied it to his pumping legs.

A tire lost the swelling at the base that indicated weight-bearing. It lifted free. Garth swerved slightly and made for the other. It leapt upward as he approached. He ran despairingly under it. Only the nose-wheel was left. Without slackening speed he rushed it. Fortunately it was smaller than the others—the rim of the wheel was only about as high as his collarbone when the tire rested on the ground. But it was off the ground when he got there. He grunted with effort and made a desperate leap.

His outthrust arm went through the lightening hole just as the wheel jerked upward. He crooked his elbow grimly as his momentum swung his flailing legs under the tire. Then he got his other arm through the hole. It was just big enough for his head and the upper part of his shoulders. The air-tanks kept him from wriggling further.

Then, to his horror, he saw the strut above him fold on a hinge.

The wheel was retractable!

He had to turn his whole body to look upward through his helmet-glass, and somehow he managed it. He had no way of gauging how deep the wheel recess was. Was it deep enough to accept the wheel—and him too?

He looked down.

It would have to be deep enough . . . the craft was a hundred feet up and rising rapidly!

He doubled up and got one toe on the edge of the lightening hole. He could just grasp the fork of the wheel. He swarmed up it, caught the other arm of the fork and lay belly down on the top part of the tire-tread. Then the wheel was inside, and the great bayflaps swung closed. The inside of the recess touched his back, squeezed, and stopped.

He couldn't move but he wasn't crushed.

It was night.

Garth crouched by a building the size of a mountain. It was built of wooden planks that looked like sections of a four-lane highway.

He tried to forget the flight, though he knew it would haunt him for years—the cramped position, the slight kink in his airhose and the large kink in his neck which had caused him such misery, and finally the horror of the landing, when the wheel he clung to had contacted and rolled. Stiff as he was, he'd had to hit the ground ahead of it and leap out of the way.

He moved along the wall, looking for a way in. He would try the doorways as a last resort, for not only were they at the top of steps with seven-foot risers but they were flooded with light.

He stumbled and fell heavily into a dark hollow scooped out at the ground line. It was about four feet deep. He got to his knees, caught a movement in the dim light, and froze. Before him was a black opening through which he could see the bright-yellow stripes of artificial light seeping between enormous floorboards. And in the dim light he was aware of something which crouched beside him in the dark. It was horny and smooth, and at one end two graceful, sensitive whips trembled and twirled.

It was a cockroach, very nearly as long as his leg.

He wet his lips. "After you, friend," he said politely.

As if it had heard him, the creature flirted its antennae and scuttled into the hole. Garth drew a deep breath and followed.

It was black and brilliant, black and brilliant under that floor. Twice he fell into holes, and one of them was wet. Filthy and determined, he explored further and further, until he lost all sense of direction. He didn't know where the entrance hole was and he no longer cared very much. He knew what he was looking for and at last he found it.

Near one wall was a considerable hump on the rough earth floor he walked on. A wide, oval patch of light above showed the presence of a tremendous knot-hole. He climbed toward it.

The wood was soft under his fingers, like balsa. He began tearing out chunks of it, widening the knot-hole. The earth here was about three feet under the hole, so he had to squat and work upward. It was extremely tiring but he kept at it until he had a hole large enough to put his head through. Because of the small size of his helmet glass, he had to put his head almost all the way up before he could see anything. And because of the brilliance above, he had to stay there a moment to accustom his eyes to the glare—What he saw made him, for the first time in his life, fully understand the phrase "And when I looked, I thought I was going to faint!"

He dropped back down the hole and lay gasping with reaction. One of the giantesses was sitting on the floor, propped up by one arm stretched out behind her. And he had busily dug his hole and thrust out his head exactly between her wide-spread thumb and forefinger!

He sat up and looked about him very carefully indeed. He followed the mammoth outline of the girl's shadow, where it crossed the lines of light between the floorboards. And then he lay back patiently to wait until she moved.

He must have dozed, and in the meantime become immune to the thunderous shuffling and subsonic bellowings of the creatures above, for when he opened his eyes again the shadow was gone. He knelt and cautiously put his head up through the hole.

The floor stretched away from him like a pampa. There were eight or nine of the huge women in the room, as far as he could see. Several were in a stage of dress which, under different circumstances, he might have found intriguing.

He pressed up harder. The tanks caught on the edge of the hole. He gritted his teeth and pushed with his legs under the floor and his arms above. He felt the wood yield under his hands. Then the tanks ripped their way through and he was at last in the room.

He backed cautiously up to the baseboard, darting glances in every direction. Making sure that none of the women was looking in his direction, he darted for the only patch of shadow he could see—a loose-hung fishnet that covered a window, serving as sort of a drape. He slid behind it and peered through the mesh. It seemed to be indifferent concealment; yet, from their point of view, he knew he would be hard to locate.

He paused to switch tanks—his air was getting foul—and then took stock.

The women were gathered around a table near the center of the room, rumbling and gesticulating in their strange, slow-motion fashion. None were looking his way. He looked down to the right. A small table stood in the corner and there was another fishnet behind it. Garth moved toward it, passing one leg which was like a redwood tree and, reaching up, twined his hands in the wide mesh of the drape. It sagged alarmingly as his weight came on it. He waited until it was still and then climbed up a few feet. Putting both feet into the mesh he jumped hard to test it. It sagged again, but held.

To the underside of the table seemed the longest thirty feet he had ever determined to travel, but he started up. The fishnet seemed to stretch a foot for every eighteen inches he climbed. He looked down and saw it touch the floor, then begin piling up.

He suddenly remembered the incredible density of the tiny Ffanx invaders, and a great light dawned in his brain.

Excitedly he climbed higher, higher, and at last reached the table top. He swung onto it, teetered for a hair-raising moment on the edge, recovered his balance, and stood on the wooden surface. Sure enough, his footprints showed on the table top as he walked away from the edge.

There was a piece of electrical equipment on the table, which he ignored. He went to the far edge, crouched by the side of the machine, and gazed across to the center table around which the giants were gathered.

His blood froze.

Under a glaring floodlight, in the center of the enormous table, lay a sealed glass cage. Lying in it, devoid of his helmet, lay Bronze's body. The leader, the one who looked so very much like Glory Gehman, was handling the delicate controls of a remote-apparatus which passed a series of rods through the pressure sleeves into the cage. At the end of the rods were clamps, clumps of white material as rough as coconut fibre, tweezers, a swab, and a gleaming scalpel as long as a two-handed sword.

If they're being that particular about atmosphere, he thought, Bronze must be alive!

The flood of joy this thought brought him died a quick death, for it was followed by . . . and they're about to vivisect him.

He yielded to a short moment of panic and despair. He rushed back toward the drape as if to slide down it and attack the women by force. He stopped, then got hold of himself.

He looked around him. Suddenly, he straightened and smiled. Then he went into furious action.

"Isn't he pretty!"

The women gathered about the tiny figure. "We shouldn't cut him up until the rest of the girls have a chance to look at him. He's just a doll!" said one.

"You've forgotten that all the Ffanx are just dolls," said the leader coolly. "Do you propose to lead thirty-two hundred women, one by one, past this little devil? You'd have a wave of hysteria I'd as soon not have to handle. Let's keep to ourselves what we have here. We'll learn what we can and file it away."

"Oh, you're so duty-bound," said the blonde petulantly. "Well, go ahead if you must."

They crowded closer. The leader propped her elbows on the table to steady her hands, and carefully manipulated the clamps. One descended over each thigh of the tiny figure and trapped it firmly to the floor of the cage. Two more captured the biceps, and another pair settled over the wrists. Then the scalpel swung up and positioned itself. The leader suddenly stopped.

"Did you leave that thing on?"

In unison they swung toward the corner. One of the women walked over and looked. "No, but the tubes are warm."

"It's a warm night," said another. "Go ahead. Cut."

They gathered about the table again. The blade turned, descended slowly.

"STOP!" roared a voice—a deep, masculine voice.

"A man!" squeaked one of the women. Another quickly drew her tunic together and belted it. A third squeaked "Where? Where? I haven't seen a man in so long I could just—"

"Glory Gehman!" said the voice. " 'Hally Gehman—short for 'Hallelujah'—remember?"

"Gesell!" gasped the leader.

"The fool," growled the blonde. "I knew a man wouldn't be able to leave us alone. This is his idea of a joke—but he set up the Gateway to play it. No wonder these little devils got through." She raised her voice. "Where are you?"

The blonde snapped her fingers. "It's a broadcast of some sort," she said. "He hasn't answered you once, Glory!" She turned to the corner. "What's my name, Dr. Gesell?"

There was a pause. Somewhere there was a squeaky sound, like the distant shattering of a field creature. "Everybody calls you Butch, towhead," said the voice. "Come over here, tapeworms."

"The recorder!"

They raced across the room, clustered around the small table.

"I thought you said it was turned off? Look—the tape's moving!" Glory reached out a hand to turn it off.

"Don't turn it off," said the voice. "Now, listen to me. You've got to believe me. I'm Gesell. No matter what you see, no matter what you think, you've got to understand that. Now, hear me out. You'll get your opportunity to test my identity after I'm finsished."

"No one but Gesell ever called me Hally," said Glory.

"Shh!" hissed the blonde.

"I'm right here in this room, and you'll see me in a moment. But before you do, Glory, I want to spout some math at you.

"Remember the vibratory interaction theory of matter? It hypothesized that universes interlock. Universe A presents itself for x duration, one cycle, then ceases to exist. Universe B replaces it; C replaces B; D replaces C, each for one micro-milli-sub-n-second of time. At the end of the chain, Universe A presents itself again. The two appearances of Universe A are consecutive in terms of an observer in Universe A. Same with B and C and all the others. Each seems to its observers to be continuous, whereas they are actually recurrent. All that's elementary.

"Here are the formulae for each theoretical universe in a limited series of four inter-recurrent continua . . ."

There followed a series of mathematical gobbledegook which was completely unintelligible to everyone in the room but Glory Gehman. She listened intently, her high-arched brows drawn together in deep thought. She drew out a tablet and stylus from her pocket and began to calculate rapidly as the voice went on.

"Now notice the quantitative shift in the first phase of each cycle. To achieve an overall resonance there has to be a shift. To put it in simple terms, if you drew an hyperbolic curve with a trembling hand, the curve is the overall resonance of the whole series of small cyclic motions. And there's only one way in which that can have a physical effect—in the continuum itself. Each cycle occurs in a slightly altered condition of space-time. That accounts for the super-density of the Ffanx and everything they owned and handled. What was normal to us was rarefied to them. We saw them as dense little androids, and they saw us as rarefied-molecule giants. There must be some point in the cycle where they are rarefied in terms of our condition. But space characteristics are only part of the continuum. The time-rate must alter with it.

"According to my calculations you have been here for something more than seven but less than eight-and-a-half months, and are waiting with considerable patience for the three-year minimum it would take to prepare the cyanide capsule for the Ffanx world.

"It's with mixed feelings that I inform you that the Ffanx war was over twenty-two earth years ago. Dr. Gilbert Gesell died in a Ffanx raid that closed the Gateway. The Gateway has been opened again momentarily but something has gone wrong with it—I don't know what. I must tell you too that in terms of Earth standards you cute cuddly creatures are in the neighborhood of seventy-five feet tall.

"So check your figures before you fly off the handle and kill any small, dense creature which arrives through a Gateway wearing a breathing helmet. It might be Dr. Gesell's little boy Garth, grown up to be all of seven inches tall, and recording into your tape at its highest speed and playing it back slowly . . ."

"I'm clinging to the fishnet just under the level of the table-top. Treat me gently, sisters. I've come a long way."

There was a concerted lunge for the drape, a concerted reaction of horror away from it. "Ffanx," someone blurted. "Kill it!"

"We have to kill it," said the blonde. "We can't take chances, Glory." Behind her voice was the concentrated horror of the conquest of Earth . . . the forcefield pens . . . the hollow, piteous presence of the handful of "returned" women. "This could be a new Ffanx trick, a new weapon . . ."

"The math is . . ."

"The hell with the math!" screamed a girl from the edge of the crowd.

"She's right!"

"She's *right!*"

"*Kill it!*"

Garth stepped over to the table top and walked toward the tape-machine. The circle of women widened instantly. Garth muscled the huge controls, placed his helmet firmly against the microphone, and chattered shrilly as the tape raced through the guides. Then he rewound, stopped the spools, and began the playback:

"I got that, and I must say I expected it. You'll follow your own consciences in the end, but be sure it's your conscience and not your panic that you follow. I want to tell you this, though: Earth is a mess. There's a new dark age back there. It's slipped into a tribal state—polyandrous in some places, feudal in others, matriarchal in many. You three thousand women, and the daughters that many of you will bear, will mean a great deal to Earth."

The chattering ran high.

"Polyandrous?"

"One woman—several husbands."

"Lead me to it! Poly wants an androus!"

"If he's seven inches high here, we'd be seventy-five feet tall there. Oh my!"

Garth's voice cut in. "You'll want to know how you can get back to Earth size, or how to get to Earth when its size corresponds to yours. I can tell you. But I'm not going to. If you can argue about my life, I can bargain with it."

A pause. "Now tell me if you've killed that boy over there." Slyly, Garth added, "Go look at him again. He's six-three, and a hundred and two percent man."

One, two, two more drifted over to the big table, to look with awed eyes at the magnificent miniature.

Glory, as if sensitive to a voice-tone she had noticed, snatched up the mike. "No, he isn't dead. He would have been, but he fired with a blaster just as I put the neo-tourmaline soaker field on him. The blaster threw out all the energy the crystal could absorb."

Garth held up his arms for the mike. When his voice came again, it said, "Glory, get together the best math minds you have here. I want to give you some raw material to work on."

There was a sudden crash of sound. To Garth it was a great thudding bass that struck at his helmet like soft-nosed bullets. To the women it was a shrill siren-alarm.

Glory yelped, "Get the 'copter warm. Asta, Marion, Josephine this time. Jo—check the transistor leads on the direction finder in the plane. It kept losing a stage of amplification this morning." She turned to the microphone. "That's a Gateway. We'll damn soon find out whether the Ffanx war is over or not. I'm going to park you with your friend there. Just pray that these cats will obey orders while I'm gone." She dropped the mike and raced to the big table. "Butch. Put that one in with the other. If you touch either one of them until I get back, so help me I'll pry you loose from your wall eyes. You hear me."

"You'll be sorry for that," snapped the blonde. "When you find out that these lousy Ffanx have been sending out a homing signal for their playmates—they're telepathic, you know—then you can apologize."

"On bended knee," said Glory. "Meantime, A-cup, do as you're told." She ran out.

"Come on. Orders is orders."

Garth watched them come. He took one step backward, then relaxed. He had shot his bolt, and all he could do was to wait. The pudgy one picked him up gingerly, tried to carry him at arm's length, found he was too heavy, and hurried across the floor with him. She set him down gently on the table. One of the women hurried up with a small edition of the cage. Garth stepped in and a gate was sealed. A tube was fitted to it, and Garth heard air hissing in. He was grateful for the increased pressure, his skin had felt raw and distended for hours.

The pudgy one lifted the small cage bodily and set it on top of the larger glass cell in which Bronze lay. A lever was flipped, and Garth dropped ungracefully into the large one.

His first act was to run to Bronze and feel his pulse. It was weak but steady. Garth unbuckled his helmet and pulled it off, then knelt by Bronze.

"Bronze . . ."

No answer.

"Bronze!"

No answer.

"Bronzie boy . . . look at all those women."

"Gug?" Bronze's eyes opened and he blinked owlishly.

Garth chuckled. "Bronze, you were after women. Look, man."

Bronze's gaze got as far as the glass wall, tested its shaky focus, and then penetrated outward. He sat bolt upright. "For me?"

Then he keeled over in a dead faint.

Garth sat and chafed his wrists, laughing weakly. Then, after a while, he went to sleep.

The pudgy one was relieved after a while. Butch waved away her own relief and stayed, elbows on the table, head low, glaring hatred and fear at the men. There was some sort of distant call. All the other women left. But the big blonde still stayed.

Garth had a dream in which he was chasing a girl in a brown cowl. She ran because she feared him, but he chased her because he knew he could show her there was nothing to fear. And as he gained on her, he heard Bronze's voice.

"Garth." It was very quiet. Intense, but weak.

Garth sat up abruptly. Something hard and sharp whacked him in the forehead. There was a gout of blood. He fell back, dazed, then opened his eyes. He saw that Butch had maneuvered the point of the scalpel within a few inches of his forehead as he slept. He could see her looking at him, her face twisted in slow-motion convulsions of laughter. The all but inaudible boom of her voice was a tangible thing, threatening the glass.

Garth turned to Bronze. He was lying on his back with one of the U-shaped clamps on his throat. It was pressing just tight enough to pin him down, just tight enough to keep his face scarlet. His breath rasped. "Garth," he whispered.

Garth staggered to his feet. Blood ran into his eyes. There was another deep hoot of laughter from outside. Garth wiped the blood away and staggered toward Bronze. The scalpel whistled down and across his path. He dodged, but lost his footing and fell.

There was a thunderous pounding on the table. Butch was apparently having herself a hell of a time.

Garth looked at the scalpel. It hung limply. He crawled toward Bronze. A tweezer-clamp shot out and caught his ankle. He pulled free of it, leaving four square inches of skin in its serrated jaws. He went on doggedly. He reached Bronze, put a foot on each side of the big man's neck, got a good grip on the U-clamp and pulled it upward. Bronze rolled free, his great lungs pumping. The flat of the scalpel hit Garth between the shoulder-blades and knocked him sprawling next to Bronze.

"How long have we been here?" asked Bronze painfully.

"Day—day and a half. On Earth, that's eight, nine months. Wonder what Viki's doing?"

He looked around, suddenly sat up. Butch was gone.

"Here come the rest of them. We'll know pretty soon."

They stood up and watched the slow, distance-eating march of the giants.

"They're carrying something . . . Will you look at those faces, Bronze!"

"They look wild."

"Glory . . . See her? The tall cool one."

"I see a tall one," said Bronze, deadpan.

"She's putting something on the big table here. Hey, what is that thing?"

"Looks like a tombstone."

Garth said, "I've heard of making the prisoner dig his
wn grave, but this—"

The stone was put in the small box and aired. Big hands
ifted it and set it on their roof.

"Get out from under."

The stone dropped, teetered. Garth leapt up and steadied
t. It settled back on its base.

It was a rough monolith, about three feet tall, cut from
oft, snow-white lime-stone. In it was a chamber with a glass
loor.

"Will you ever look at that," breathed Bronze.

Garth stared.

Cut into the stone were the words,

THE GATEWAY
OF
GESELL

"I don't get it," said Garth.

Bronze said, "Look in the thing. The little door."

Garth peered, and saw a plastic scroll. He opened the
door, took out the scroll and unrolled it. In exquisitely neat
script it read:

> This is your Gateway to all that is human;
> to all that sweats, and cries, and tries;
> to all hungers, to all puzzlement;
> to mistakes compounded,
> to mysteries cleared,
> to growth, to strength, to complication,
> to ultimate simplicity.
> Friends, be welcome,
> others be warned.
> Gesell is your gate
> As he was mine.
> A closed gate should never be guarded.
> My gate is open, I guard it well.
>> Gesell knows I love him.
>> Please tell him I know it too.
>>> Viki (Escaped)

There was a long quiet.

"Escaped," said Garth. "Escaped."

There was a thump over their heads. The airlock box
had been placed there. There was a speaker baffle into it.
It dropped. Bronze caught it, handed it to Garth.

Garth looked out through the wall and saw Glory, her calm face suffused, her eyes misty.

"Garth Gesell, you've read the scroll. I brought it because I didn't want you to wait; I didn't want you to just hear about it. She fixed your Gateway, Garth, and shoved the stone through so we'd find it. Then, when we were whooping and bawling properly, she let us find her.

"We couldn't have trusted any calculations, any statements. But we examined her and she's Escaped—oh, beyond question. That we could trust. For the one thing the Ffanx would never spend, not even to bait a trap for the biggest game, was a single drop of extradiol, which she carries unmolested. Viki's given us back a world, Garth, just by loving you . . .

"Are you ready to start on the calculations?"

Garth leaned against the wall near the speaker. Standing upright seemed to make his heart labor. "Not until I've seen Viki," he said.

There was a pause. Then Glory's voice again, "Bronze. Put on that helmet."

Unquestioningly, Bronze did. The airlock box thumped above them. Garth sat down and leaned against the wall. His heart would not be quiet.

Bronze was suddenly beside him, helmeted. He clasped Garth's shoulder so hard it hurt, and as suddenly was gone. There was a slight scuffling sound. Garth turned. Bronze, in the lock, was lowering someone into the cage. Then the upper box was taken away.

She stood and looked at him gravely, unafraid. But this time there was a world of difference.

He put out his arms. He, or she, moved. Perhaps both. He pressed her cheek against his, and when he took it away, both were wet. So one of them wept.

Perhaps both.

With her mathematical staff, Glory said, "He was quite right about the shift, you see. He and Viki and Bronze can go back through their own Gateway. But we'll have to open another. We go to a world where we will be only three times the size of the natives. There we build still another Gateway. And that will be Earth, and we'll be home."

"If it's as easy as that," asked the pudgy one, "Why did we have to be so cautious? Why didn't we go straight to that intermediate world and wait there?"

"Because," said Glory Gehman, "the intermediate world s the Ffanx planet. Do you see?"

Earth keeps a solemn festival at the meadows of Hack nd Sack, through whose blue arch came first death, and 1en life.

THE END

Are you missing out on some great Jove/HBJ books?

"You can have any title in print at Jove/HBJ delivered right to your door! To receive your Jove/HBJ Shop-At-Home Catalog, send us 25¢ together with the label below showing your name and address.

JOVE PUBLICATIONS, INC.
Harcourt Brace Jovanovich, Inc.
Dept. M.O., 757 Third Avenue, New York, N.Y. 10017

NAME_____

ADDRESS_____

CITY_____STATE_____

NT-1   ZIP_____